ALSO BY CHRISTINA USS

The Adventures of a Girl Called Bicycle
The Colossus of Roads

A Few
BICYCLES
More

Christina Uss

Margaret Ferguson Books

Holiday House • New York

Margaret Ferguson Books

Library of Congress Cataloging-in-Publication Data

Names: Uss, Christina, author.
Title: A few bicycles more / by Christina Uss.
Description: First edition. | New York : Margaret Ferguson Books/Holiday
House, [2022] | Audience: Ages 8 to 12. | Audience: Grades 4-6.
Summary: Twelve-year-old Bicycle's trusty bike Fortune takes them to
Harpers Ferry, West Virginia, where she reunites with her long-lost
family and hatches a plan to share her love of cycling with her new sisters.
Identifiers: LCCN 2021054993 | ISBN 9780823450879 (hardcover)
Subjects: CYAC: Bicycles and bicycling—Fiction. | Quintuplets—Fiction.
Sisters—Fiction. | Adventure and adventurers—Fiction. | Harpers Ferry
(W. Va.)—Fiction. | LCGFT: Novels.
Classification: LCC PZ7.1.U86 Fe 2022 | DDC [Fic]—dc23
LC record available at https://lccn.loc.gov/2021054993

ISBN: 978-0-8234-5087-9 (hardcover)

To my own Egg and Drumstick

CONTENTS

A Few
BICYCLES
More

MORE UNUSUAL THAN USUAL

The Wheels of Fortune 713-J was no ordinary bike.

To defend its rider, it could shoot rubber snakes like missiles. To feed its rider, it produced something that looked (but didn't taste) like a Tootsie Roll. Tucked neatly inside its seat post, it hid a tent with built-in air-conditioning. With the touch of a button, it could produce maps or play any kind of music you wanted to listen to. It printed money, planned getaways, and was learning how to tell knock-knock jokes. Every bike has a personality, but the Fortune was in a class by itself.

On this Friday afternoon, though, the Fortune was acting more unusual than usual. It was insisting that its owner, a twelve-year-old girl called Bicycle, pedal the wrong way.

TURN RIGHT, it blinked in large letters on its computer screen.

They were on a paved trail a few miles from their

neighborhood in Washington, D.C., where people liked to ride and jog. To their right rippled the Potomac River. The Potomac wasn't some little creek. If Bicycle turned right, *plop* and *swoosh*: she and the Fortune would be underwater. She wasn't about to do something as silly as that. Ever since earning her name by saying "bicycle" as her first and most-frequently-used word, Bicycle was destined to go everywhere on two wheels. She was an excellent rider.

"Is this a joke? Because I think you're better off with the knock-knock kind," Bicycle said.

The Fortune was still figuring out what made jokes funny. Its last one was: Knock knock. *Who's there?* A man knocking at the door. *A man knocking at the door who?* His name is Edward. It hadn't gotten the hang of them yet.

TURN RIGHT, the computer screen blinked again.

"There's no road there, Fortune," Bicycle explained for the second time. The bike had started blinking like this three blocks earlier. "No bridge, no path, no nothing. There's just water. I'm turning left and heading home." They'd gone for a ride after Bicycle finished her homeschool lessons, and the day was edging toward dinnertime.

It crossed her mind that maybe the Fortune was acting weird because it was bored. She'd had the great good luck to buy the Fortune this past summer, thinking it was a snazzy racing bike. It had proved to be more than snazzy. It had become Bicycle's friend, doing its best to help her when she needed it—and since they'd biked together across the United States and back again, she'd needed it a lot.

However, she hadn't needed the tent or any of the other fancy features since they'd returned to Washington, D.C., a month ago. Bicycle had needed a break from epic adventuring, so they'd only taken short rides to familiar places. Maybe this whole "turn right" bit was her bike's way of asking for more excitement in their daily rides.

She had an idea. "I'm still not up for any major adventures, but I'll tell you what—I promise we will try practicing wheelies when we get to our driveway."

TURN RIGHT, the display blinked again, this time in bold. **RIGHT RIGHT RIGHT RIGHT RIGHT.** An alarm started going off. The Fortune had an array of different alarms, including a police-siren wail, a school-bell clang, and a howler-monkey yawp. It was using the yawp of a king-size howler monkey. People jogging nearby turned to glare at them.

"Hey. Hey! Why are you doing that?" Bicycle asked, pressing its buttons and hoping one was the alarm's off switch. The Fortune had a ton of buttons, and Bicycle still didn't know what they all did. She hit each of them at least once, but it didn't make any difference. "Fortune, help me out here!"

The alarm was replaced by a piece of gospel music blaring at top volume. The singers warbled about being taken to the river. When they hit a high note, the music stopped as abruptly as it began.

The Fortune's display went blank for a long moment before it blinked, I am sorry. I did not pick the music, nor did I intend to make so much noise. I also did not choose to tell you to turn right, since right was clearly wrong.

"Did your computer overheat or something?" It was warm for a mid-October day. Bicycle thought anyone might act obnoxiously when they got too hot. She got pretty grouchy herself without shade and cool drinks.

I do not know.

Bicycle knew the Fortune did not like admitting it didn't know something, so she chose not to make a big deal out of it. "Probably some kind of temporary electronic burp, nothing to worry about. We'll go home and I'll give you a quick rinse with the hose. That'll cool you down." She pushed a pedal forward, turned left, and was relieved to see the Fortune's display get back to normal with sensible directions.

We have a light tailwind from the west. It is 3.14159 miles to the Mostly Silent Monastery, so we will be home in 11.78 minutes.

Mostly Silent Monasteries and their sister organizations, Nearly Silent Nunneries, are found in most U.S. states and around the world. They welcome members of the public to come in whenever they need someone to listen to them.

4

Mostly Silent Monks and Nearly Silent Nuns are trained to be the best possible listeners. They pay attention with their whole selves and talk as little as necessary. They haven't taken vows of complete silence like some folks do because their founders thought that being 100 percent silent would make it awfully hard to be polite, or to be safe, or to get something to eat when they were hungry. Thus, they've taken vows never to say more than the Sacred Eight Words: "yes," "no," "maybe," "now," "later," "sleep," "help," and "sandwich." It isn't easy, but providing listening ears for the world's worries and wonderings is worth it.

Bicycle had appeared on the steps of D.C.'s Mostly Silent Monastery as a toddler. The monks hadn't been able to find out where she belonged, so they'd kept her and raised her. This might have been a tragic origin story for another child, but life is what you make of it. She was happy to call the peaceful place her home.

Bicycle coasted up the driveway and across the grass to the shed where the monks kept tools and gardening equipment. She parked the Fortune and unwound the hose, turning the nozzle on medium to give the bike's frame a thorough rinse.

"Doesn't that feel better?" she asked the Fortune as she sluiced away a small dollop of mud.

Yes, thank you. Knock knock.

"Who's there?"

Harp music began blasting out of the Fortune's speakers. One doesn't ordinarily think of harp music as harsh, but it can be if played loudly enough.

Oh dear.

The Top Monk's head, covered with a wide-brimmed sun hat, popped up between the kale plants in the garden. Bicycle hadn't noticed him there. He was the most Mostly Silent of all the Mostly Silent Monks, having reduced his entire vocabulary down to one single word from the Sacred Eight. That word was "sandwich."

"Sandwich?" he yelled over the din.

Bicycle knew from his tone and his facial expression that he meant, "As much as I enjoy listening to music, that is a smidgen too loud. Would you be so kind as to turn it down?"

"Sandwich!" she called back, trying to get across the meaning of "No problem!"

The Top Monk raised an eyebrow at her. She'd need a lot more practice before she'd have his kind of mastery over the Sacred Eight Words.

She placed her palm on the bike's handlebars and asked, "Can you please cut that out?"

No. Yes. Maybe?

Instead of stopping abruptly like it had before, the volume of the harp music gradually decreased into silence. Bicycle could feel the bike trembling with the effort.

"It was just the shock of the cold water," she said, even

though she had no idea if this was true. Bicycle gave the frame one last pass with the hose, then polished it dry with a rag from the shed. "I'll take you upstairs for a rest. Come on." She rolled the Fortune in the back door of the monastery and headed to their room.

Once the Fortune was leaning on its kickstand by the window, Bicycle sat down at her tiny desk. She pulled out her book on bike repair, pawing past the bits she already knew by heart. She scanned the index and flipped to the page that dealt with bike computers, speedometers, and odometers. The only advice it offered when a bike computer was acting wonky was to replace its battery. Bicycle glanced at the Fortune. She thought about how she'd like to be treated if she were burping out alarms and music without meaning to. Would she want someone asking questions about her batteries or prying in to replace them? She didn't think so.

The past summer, Bicycle had made her first friends when cycling across the United States. She'd had to figure out some rules about friend-making. She knew she needed to start by saying something nice and listening carefully to what any potential friend said back. She had also learned that there was an element of mystery to friendship, and that one never knew where or how it might sprout—even between a girl and a bike with artificial intelligence.

Her group of new friends was scattered across the country, so the Fortune was the only one she saw every day.

Maybe she'd have to come up with some rules about how to take care of a friendship when a friend started acting abnormally odd and loud.

She decided to give the Fortune some space. "I'm going to go see if the monks need any help with dinner," she said.

An extra pair of hands was always welcome in the monastery kitchen. Bicycle joined the ranks at the cutting boards and chopped kale and sweet potatoes for a pot of vegetable soup big enough to feed sixty. Then she enjoyed a mostly silent meal and a mostly silent game of cards, after which she curled up in complete silence to read in bed.

YAWP YAWP YAWP YAWP—the Fortune's howler-monkey alarm went off in the dead of night. Bicycle herself yawped in surprise and got tangled in her bedsheets. Before she could get loose, her door flew open. In burst Sister Wanda.

Sister Wanda was Bicycle's chief guardian and teacher. She'd retired years ago from following her Nearly Silent vow and was now the Mostly Silent Monastery's manager. She made sure that supplies were ordered, bills were paid, and daily operations ran properly. She had no qualms about using her voice to get control of a situation.

"What is the meaning of this?" Sister Wanda roared, turning on the light. She was brandishing a vase of flowers with a take-no-prisoners look in her eyes. She zeroed in on the Fortune. "Stop that this instant!"

The Fortune went on howling. This was serious. The Fortune did not disobey Sister Wanda if it could help it. No one did. Bicycle managed to unravel herself enough from her sheets to hop to the Fortune's side.

"You're okay, you're okay," she said, covering both ears with her hands and trying to press buttons with her elbow. She mashed down four of them together, and the bike began playing the same gospel music as before. A group of concerned monks in pajamas crowded around the door with their fingers plugging their ears, murmuring, "Help?"

The gospel music was an improvement, but it was still ear-splitting. Sister Wanda shot a stern look at Bicycle; Bicycle shook her head in bewilderment.

Sister Wanda handed the vase of flowers to the nearest monk. "Bicycle, bring your bike down to the laundry room. Everyone else, go to the linen storage closet, grab as many winter quilts as you can and meet us downstairs."

Bicycle hoisted the Fortune onto one shoulder. She needed both hands for this, so she commanded the muscles in her ears to pinch themselves closed. She contorted her face, trying to figure out if ears even had any muscles inside them. They didn't seem to. She carried her friend to the laundry room and hoped her hearing would survive.

When the Fortune was parked in front of the washers and dryers, Sister Wanda directed the monks to cover the bike in thick comforter after thick comforter. The nun grilled Bicycle about the cause of the hullaballoo, and Bicycle described the strange afternoon.

Sister Wanda said, "It sounds like I should call the doctor in the morning." She corrected herself. "That is, I will call the bike mechanic." Anyone who knew the bike well found it hard to remember that it wasn't alive. "We may have to go to the computer repair shop as well, or the electronics store that sells speakers. . . ."

Bicycle felt her shoulders relax as Sister Wanda made her to-do list for the following day. No problem would dare stand in the nun's way for long.

After eleven cozy layers, the gospel music finally became bearable. The Fortune didn't even resemble a bike anymore, just a large, snug, faintly singing lump. The Top Monk tucked in the edge of the top layer while everyone else began heading back upstairs.

Bicycle hung back, feeling like she ought to do something, but with her mind sleep-fuzzed and her body calling for bed, she had no idea what. When she finally mounted the stairs, she noticed the Top Monk standing very still with his hand resting against the comforters. He quietly sang back to the swaddled bike, "Sa-ha-hand-wi-i-ich."

Bicycle was pretty sure he meant, *I hear you.*

She thought, *So do I. So did everyone tonight, whether they wanted to or not.* Then she remembered she hadn't practiced popping wheelies in the driveway as she'd promised.

She didn't know if her bike had even wanted to. She was sure she could be a better friend than that.

Tomorrow, things will get fixed so that I can not only hear the Fortune but also take the time to listen to it without my ears falling off.

TURN RIGHT. TURN RIGHT. TURN RIGHT.

The next morning, Bicycle plodded downstairs, not at her most bright-eyed and bushy-tailed. She found the Fortune still broadcasting music from underneath its pile of comforters. It had gone back to playing harp melodies like the one that had startled the Top Monk in the garden. The monks assigned to laundry duty were humming along.

Sister Wanda joined Bicycle and brought her to the kitchen. "Get some breakfast into yourself, child. We have an appointment at the Wheel World Bike Shop this morning. The owner assured me he's the best mechanic in the city and that there's no bike he can't fix. We'll see." She looked skeptically at the blanket lump. "It was playing pop music before, 'Ticket on a Ferry Ride' by the Monkees. Has it switched to harp now? There's no telling what might come next. Maybe I should go scare up something to use as earplugs for both of us."

"Earplugs would be great," Bicycle said. While she ate her bowl of oatmeal, she considered the training she'd received from the monks on how to listen. Had anyone ever said anything about how to temporarily reverse the process and *not* listen to something? She couldn't think of a single bit of sound-ignoring advice. When Sister Wanda offered her the choice between a pair of earmuffs and some foam plugs, she decided she needed all the help she could get and took both.

Sister Wanda arranged for Brother Otto to answer the phones for her while they were gone. Talkative Brother Otto had been deeply relieved when, several months ago, he'd been absolved of his vows so he could help Sister Wanda in her duties.

Bicycle and Sister Wanda excavated the Fortune from the comforters and took it outside to the driveway. The bike was still playing the harp music without pause. It belted out a lullaby in the driveway that was so loud it probably woke up sleeping babies across the city.

Bicycle yelled to the Fortune in what she hoped was a reassuring tone of voice, but it was hard to yell and not sound upset. "Okay, we're going to the bike shop now to get this fixed!" She told it the address.

The Fortune found it in its database and displayed a map and directions: 6.28318 miles to the Wheel World Bike Shop.

She patted it.

Wearing her black exercise robe and leggings—along with a pair of leopard-print earmuffs—Sister Wanda sat astride her elderly bike. She gestured to Bicycle to lead the way. As they rode down the street, people came out of their houses to see what the noise was. Kids waved and leaned sideways to look down the road behind them.

One boy called out, "What's the parade for? And where's the rest of it?"

His words were muffled by the earplugs and earmuffs, but Bicycle heard him. She shouted back, "We're just riding our bikes!" She tried not to be embarrassed by the attention and focused on pushing the pedals and following the directions. They headed west, not far from the trail where she'd been riding the Fortune the day before.

When they got within a few blocks of the Potomac River, the Fortune stopped playing the harp music. Bicycle looked down at its screen. It was flashing TURN RIGHT in big letters. This time, turning right would lead them smack into the side of a brick wall.

"Not again," she said under her breath. She was glad the bike shop was less than half a mile away.

She turned the handlebars to the left. But they wouldn't go. Instead, the brakes squeezed themselves under her hand. The pedals slowed themselves under her feet. The Fortune came to a dead stop. It had never taken over control of itself like this before, not in thousands of miles of riding together.

"Whoa!" Sister Wanda exclaimed as she narrowly avoided crashing into the two of them. "Remember to signal when you're stopping!"

"I didn't know we were stopping. The Fortune stopped itself," Bicycle said. She didn't want to block traffic, so she dismounted her bike and lifted it onto the sidewalk. "What is going on?" she asked it, hoping it wouldn't keep blinking TURN RIGHT in reply.

The Fortune let out a blast of rock music. The Beatles started repeating the word "Help!" over and over out of its speakers. Sister Wanda brought her bike up on the sidewalk as well.

"Help's right around the next corner," Bicycle said to the Fortune through the rising niggle of a headache. "Do you want me to carry you there?"

I am not asking for help. I am still not controlling the music. I do not know what is.

"Maybe you're picking up radio stations?" Sister Wanda asked.

No. It feels like a magnet is pulling these songs out of my database and forcing them to play. The magnet is also trying to pull me into a brick wall.

"I bet the bike mechanic has never had a problem like this to fix before," said Bicycle.

It is very uncomfortable. TURN RIGHT. TURN RIGHT. TURN RIGHT.

Sister Wanda said, "We need to get you to the mechanic with all haste."

Bicycle agreed. She gently placed the Fortune over one shoulder and carried it to the corner, where she and Sister Wanda turned left.

As soon as they stepped into the crosswalk, the Fortune's blasting music changed. This next song was country-and-western-style guitar accompanying a singer crooning about mountains and trees and country roads taking him home to West Virginia. Bicycle gritted her teeth and kept moving until they found the Wheel World Bike Shop. Sister Wanda held the door open, and Bicycle walked partway through.

The owner came around the bike stand where he was working and waved a pedal wrench at her. "No one comes into my shop singing John Denver songs, nope! Stop that racket!"

"I'm sorry, sir!" Bicycle yelled back in as friendly a way as she could. "I'm not singing it! It's my bike, you see—"

"Don't care where it's coming from, only care that it stops!" He raised his eyebrows and waited for quiet. "Not willing to abide by my rules? Then out you go!" He advanced on Bicycle and she stepped outside.

"Now, see here—" Sister Wanda began, but the mechanic grabbed the door handle and slammed the door shut, turning the lock with a stubborn jut of his jaw. He flipped the OPEN sign to CLOSED and retreated back to his bike stand. "Well, I never," said Sister Wanda.

Bicycle's headache was growing from a little niggle into a throb between her eyes. She took the Fortune off her shoulder and shouted, "What do we do now?"

Sister Wanda shouted back, "I'd give that mechanic a piece of my mind, but he wouldn't hear a word. We'll try a computer repair store and hope for a better welcome."

The employee who greeted them at Hackers, Inc., was considerably more gracious than the bike mechanic. Her name tag read HEAD HACKER. She said she didn't mind the music since she usually listened to loud tunes through her earbuds when she was fixing things. Bicycle told her about the glitches the Fortune had experienced, including the ones on the morning's ride.

"Even if you can do no more than get the volume down, we will be grateful," Sister Wanda added.

The Head Hacker promised to see what she could do, and asked if they could leave the bike for the rest of the weekend for her to run a full diagnostic test.

"Sure!" said Bicycle lickety-split, thinking of going home for a nap to cancel out her headache. She then hoped the Fortune didn't notice how eagerly she'd answered. It was hard to tell—the music kept on pouring out in waves of two-part harmony. She gave her bike a hug and explained that they'd be back to pick it up on Monday.

She climbed aboard Sister Wanda's rear rack for the ride

home. Even when they were far from Hackers, Inc., she kept the earmuffs on.

The rest of the weekend was mostly silent. No adventures were had. Nothing unexpected happened. Bicycle felt guilty about how much she enjoyed it. She'd left her friend, who clearly wasn't well, somewhere unfamiliar and hadn't even asked about coming to visit to check up on it. This might turn out to be a good rule of friendship: Try Not to Be Selfish, Even When Your Head Hurts.

The Head Hacker called on Monday during homeschool time. Sister Wanda put her on speakerphone in the monastery office.

"I've got some good news and some bad news," the Head Hacker said. "Which do you want first?"

"The bad news," Bicycle answered. In her opinion, get the bad news out of the way first, and hold the good news in reserve like an antidote.

"I couldn't fix the Fortune. I barely understood its programming language. You have one complicated bike. I couldn't even reboot it—and when I tried, it told me to please stop because I was tickling it. It also told me some knock-knock jokes, but I didn't get the punch lines."

"That part's normal," Bicycle assured her. It made her feel better to know the mysterious magnetic force hadn't sucked away the Fortune's sense of humor, such as it was.

"What's the good news?" asked Sister Wanda.

"Well, I took it for a ride. I hope you don't mind, but my coworkers asked me to give them a break from the music. I like to ride this trail that parallels a canal next to the Potomac River in Georgetown. It's called the Chesapeake and Ohio Canal Towpath, the C&O for short, so I took your bike over there. As soon as I hit the C&O, everything got quieter. Here, listen."

The Head Hacker must have held her phone up toward the Fortune. Bicycle could hear the country roads song, faintly.

"Oh, thank Saint Euphemia and all her silent sisters," said Sister Wanda.

The Head Hacker continued, "One more thing you should know. When I tried to ride back to my office, the volume went crazy again and the bike kept blinking at me to turn around. So as long as you don't ride your bike anywhere but on the towpath, I guess you're in good shape. In fact, would you mind meeting me here to pick it up? I said that my coworkers asked me to give them a break, but it's more true to say that they threw me out and locked the door. I'm right near a coffeeshop." She rattled off the name and address.

"Ah. Well, that will be fine. We will be there shortly. Goodbye," Sister Wanda said.

She and Bicycle looked at each other.

The nun tapped her fingers on the table. "It sounds like

your bike isn't quite ready to come home, but it can't stay where it is. This is a pickle."

Bicycle thought about how the Fortune had said it felt like a magnet was trying to pull it into the Potomac River. The Head Hacker had said that the towpath ran parallel to a canal that had been dug next to the Potomac River. "Maybe we should try taking a ride on the C&O Canal Towpath and see what happens," Bicycle suggested. Heading who-knew-how-far to find who-knew-what didn't sound great. However, here was an opportunity to practice being an unselfish friend. "If you're too busy, I can go alone," she offered.

"Not on my watch." Sister Wanda looked at the civics textbook on her desk. "I suppose taking advantage of a nice day to do our lessons from the seats of our bikes wouldn't be the worst idea. You're lucky to have a teacher who can instruct you about the Bill of Rights off the top of her head." She checked her watch. "Please go get your backpack and fill it with some wholesome snacks and two water bottles. I can have Brother Otto cover for me while we're gone. I hate to say this, but if we haven't solved things by dinnertime, you'll have to brush up on your sewing skills for Plan B."

"Which is?" Bicycle said.

"Plan B is you sewing an eleven-comforter-thick muffler for the Fortune to wear over its speakers when we get home."

Bicycle wasn't very good at sewing. She pictured herself

toiling away at the sewing machine so that the Fortune could end up partially swallowed by fabric like some unrideable thing that was half-bike, half-marshmallow. Wait, was she thinking selfishly? This was tricky. Where was the line between being selfish and being herself? She hoped doing something she *was* good at—cycling—would solve the Fortune's problem, and Plan B wouldn't happen.

She went to hunt for some wholesome-ingredient-type muffins in the monastery kitchen to power her and Sister Wanda's pedaling.

TURN LEFT

Bicycle sat piggyback on Sister Wanda's rear bike rack as the nun maneuvered them through light traffic to Schlagobers Café, the coffeeshop where the Head Hacker was waiting. They found her holding a cup of hot chocolate and sitting on the stoop outside next to the less-noisy Fortune. She pointed them toward a paved path bordering a waterway. This waterway wasn't the rippling Potomac River, but a narrow canal contained by stone walls.

"That's where your bike seems happiest. Sorry I couldn't help you more."

"You've given us a place to start," Sister Wanda told her. "Sometimes, that's all one needs."

Bicycle thanked the Head Hacker, got onto the Fortune, and headed off with Sister Wanda. Once they started to pedal, Bicycle launched into a series of questions. "Fortune, can you still feel the magnet pulling you? Are we going the right way? How far do you think the magnet wants you to go? Can you tell what it is? Should we look for radio towers? Or giant U-shaped magnets like they draw in cartoons?" Since she could now listen to her bike without her ears falling off, Bicycle wanted some answers.

Yes. Yes. I can't tell. I can't tell. Perhaps. Perhaps. The Fortune was still playing the same country music that had so irritated the bike mechanic.

Bicycle eyed the shallow water next to the trail. The canal was about as wide as a two-lane road. "You said before it was telling you to go into the river. Is it still trying to make you dunk yourself underwater here?"

No. I do not feel I must submerge myself. It seems to be enough that we are now closely following the path of the Potomac River northeast. The Fortune reached the chorus of the song about country roads taking it home to West Virginia.

Sister Wanda surprised Bicycle by singing along in a clear soprano voice. "Until it was playing at a manageable volume, I couldn't remember that I liked this song."

"You and the monks always taught me that listening properly meant being sensitive to small details, but you never said what to do if you end up hit by huge sounds."

"Sometimes we have desperate folks coming in to the Mostly Silent Monastery who talk very fast and very passionately. The monks are trained to catch it all in their minds like they're corralling thrashing fish into separate ponds, giving the words a chance to settle down so they can pay attention to each one. . . ." Sister Wanda gave the Fortune a thoughtful look. "What songs has your bike been playing? Are they all different, or is it repeating some of them?"

"Repeating them, as far as I can tell," Bicycle said. She asked the Fortune if it could make a list of the songs it had been compelled to play. It displayed:

> Take Me to the River
> Harp-A-Palooza
> Ticket on a Ferry Ride
> Help!
> Take Me Home, Country Roads

She read the list to Sister Wanda.

"I wonder if that's the jumbled pile of nonsense it seems at first glance," said the nun. "Perhaps these songs are clues to where the Fortune is being pulled. Let's see, we've got rivers, harps—perhaps that refers to 'harping upon' something, which means to speak persistently about a certain topic until it becomes tiresome. 'Harp' is also slang for a harmonica." As far as anyone could tell, Sister Wanda knew everything about everything. "The ferry song might also refer to rivers and how to cross them. I believe there are water taxis still in operation on the Potomac. Then there's the call for help, and asking for country roads to lead one home. . . . Hmm."

The paved path joined a well-packed crushed-gravel trail. This was one of the places in the city where you could learn about history as you exercised. Every quarter mile or so, Bicycle started to notice placards, statues, and markers. One she could read from afar said BUILDING THE C&O CANAL 1828–1831. A lot of old railroad beds in the United States had been turned into trails because they provided long, flat stretches for walking and cycling separate from cars. This particular one hadn't been part of the railroad system but had instead been trodden by horses and oxen towing barges up and down the waterway. Wherever the Fortune was being pulled, at least the path to get there was flat. For now.

Bicycle's eyes were drawn to the Fortune's list of song titles displayed on its screen. She liked making anagrams, rearranging letters to find new words hiding inside existing words. It was best when you could mix up every one of the letters into a whole new phrase or word, like making the letters in LISTEN spell SILENT. She could see right away that "Harp-A-Palooza" had POOL, LOOP, and POLAR in it. She got suspicious for a moment. She asked the Fortune, "You're sure this isn't a joke or some kind of puzzle you made up, where Sister Wanda and I have to solve clues and you pretend you don't know what's going on?"

I would never pretend that. I don't like not knowing what is going on.

Bicycle decided that sounded true. She went back to anagram-searching. "Harp-A-Palooza" also had ALOHA. Another song, "Ticket on a Ferry Ride," had EATEN, CAKE, and TACO buried inside. After some deep focus, she found that "Take Me to the River" had the word METEORITE in it. She grinned. An eight-letter word was anagram treasure.

Sister Wanda broke Bicycle's letter-mixing reverie. "If there is a clue in those song choices, it isn't particularly obvious. We may be looking for a ferry boat carrying harmonicas or an orchestra with harps that plays riverside concerts. Neither of which makes much sense. Have you any ideas?"

"Do meteorites have magnetic properties?" Bicycle asked.

"Most contain some sort of metal like iron, so they will attract magnets but not exert a magnetic pull. I feel confident that if a meteorite had fallen to Earth recently with enough magnetized material to call attention to itself, I would have read about it in the newspaper." Sister Wanda addressed the Fortune. "Come now, your database is as wide as it is deep. Can you contribute any helpful suggestions?"

The country music was replaced by the harp music, which then switched after a few bars to "Ticket on a Ferry Ride" and then back to "Take Me Home, Country Roads." It started playing these same three snippets on a loop. It was like listening to a radio when someone kept flicking the dial around to different stations without being able to choose what they wanted.

"I will be frank with you. That is just as annoying as the loud music," Sister Wanda informed the Fortune.

I am sorry. I still do not have control.

Sister Wanda sighed and signaled that she was coasting to a stop and pulling off the trail. Bicycle joined her.

"Let's have a look-see at this trail map," Sister Wanda said. "If a ferryboat sank with a load of harmonicas in this canal, I'm sure there will be a historic marker saying so."

The map showed upcoming campsites, boat launches, restrooms, river dams, and canal locks. It also informed them that this trail was 184.5 miles long and would take them as far as Cumberland, Maryland. Bicycle let out a low whistle. "That's a long way to look for sunken harmonicas or freshly fallen meteorites."

"With a stop for lunch, if the trail is flat the whole way," Sister Wanda mused, "fifty miles would be a reasonable distance for us today."

Not for the first time, Bicycle wondered about her guardian's age. She had a cap of silver hair and wrinkles around her eyes and mouth, but she could pedal a bike at a steady speed forever and a day.

"There's a Nearly Silent Nunnery in Harpers Ferry where we can spend the night. It's about fifty miles away."

One of the nice features of Mostly Silent Monasteries and Nearly Silent Nunneries was that they kept bedrooms available for travelers in need of peace and quiet for a night.

The Fortune called up its own map and blinked Harpers Ferry, West Virginia, is 51.94247 miles from here. Light winds from the south. We can be there well before dinnertime. I can provide lunch.

It popped out two Complete Nutrition pellets from its handlebar end, which Bicycle caught and stuffed into her pocket. She'd eaten these brown, oily-flavored niblets to survive when food was scarce before. She knew that if any other lunch option existed along their route, she and Sister Wanda would prefer the other option, no matter what it was.

They got back on the trail. "The best we can do is to keep our eyes peeled for anything peculiar. Especially you, Mr. Fancy Bike." This was what Sister Wanda called the Fortune when she was lecturing it. "Stay alert, and let us know the instant you notice something that might make sense of your troubles."

I will do my best.

Sister Wanda launched into a lesson on the first ten amendments to the U.S. Constitution and why they were deemed the Bill of Rights. Bicycle had to admit she wasn't learning much; she kept getting distracted by their stops to read historical markers, plus the Fortune's loop of harp-and-ferry music.

The trail was a bit rocky and muddy in places, but all in all it was a nice ride. Lots of shade. Fall had barely arrived down in D.C., but the farther north they got, the more the trees committed to showing oranges and yellows.

In fact, mostly what they saw were trees. Also views of the canal, which was full of water in some places and dry in others. After their fifth stop to read a marker, Sister Wanda abandoned the civics lesson and instead wove historical facts into a spontaneous lesson on American modes of transportation in the early 1800s. Nothing they saw struck them as peculiar.

As they got closer and closer to the end of the day, Bicycle felt worse and worse for the Fortune. She felt especially bad when Sister Wanda told it with barely disguised exasperation, "I will personally clean and oil every link of your chain if you can play any other song ever written by any other musician, anywhere, at any time in the history of humanity."

Five minutes later, the bike played the opening to Johnny Cash's "Folsom Prison Blues."

"Ha!" Sister Wanda exhaled in surprise. "I didn't think that would work. I'll scrub your chain spick-and-span when we return home."

"Good job, Fortune," Bicycle told it.

It was not a good job. The music changed on its own without my control.

Bicycle listened to Johnny Cash's mellow voice sing

about a prisoner tortured by hearing a train rolling along outside his cell. She wondered if the Fortune was feeling tortured by this magnetic pull.

Sister Wanda slowed as they approached a metal staircase leading to a bridge. The bridge had room for pedestrians on one side and train tracks on the other. A blue-and-yellow freight train was clacking across the river. "That bridge leads to Harpers Ferry and West Virginia," Sister Wanda told the Fortune, "so unless you have any suggestions, this is the end of our search for today."

The train's whistle blew, echoing over the water.

The Fortune blinked its display in rhythm with Johnny Cash's voice telling everyone that when he heard that train whistle blowing, he'd hang his head and cry. Then it let out a long, triumphant *boooop*. I calculate that there is an 82.46% chance that I have solved the puzzle. One possible interpretation of the songs I have played by harpers and about ferries and country roads in West Virginia is that the magnetic force wanted to pull me to Harpers Ferry, West Virginia.

Sister Wanda smacked her forehead. "Why didn't I think of that?"

"That's pretty good interpreting," said Bicycle. "But who or what sent you a music puzzle to bring you here?"

I believe there is only one way to find out. Turn right.

SEEING MORE THAN DOUBLE

The Fortune kept playing "Folsom Prison Blues" as they crossed the bridge and rode onto the main street of the small town of Harpers Ferry. It was a cheery-looking place, tucked in the shadow of some wooded hills, full of tidy eighteenth-century buildings, souvenir shops, and restaurants. Bicycle began to slow down when she saw an ice cream parlor, but the Fortune blinked, Keep going, please.

The road climbed and descended, and the historic stone and brick homes gave way to more industrial-looking structures. They saw a marker indicating they'd entered West Harpers Ferry. This town put on nowhere near as cheerful a face to the world. Gated driveways, smokestacks, and a lot of chain-link fences dominated the roadside of West Harpers Ferry.

After listening to the sixth mournful rendition of "Folsom Prison Blues," Bicycle murmured nervously to the

Fortune, "What does this new song mean? Are we going to a prison?"

The Fortune abruptly went silent. It blinked, The pull is gone.

Bicycle asked, "Like we've found its source?" There was nothing much around them.

No. It seemed to switch off like a light. Turn back.

Bicycle told Sister Wanda they needed to retrace their steps. They headed back the way they'd come, more slowly this time, checking both sides of the road for mysteries.

Stop. This is the place I last felt the pull.

"The place" was about the last place Bicycle would have hoped to stop. The chain-link fence here was topped with a layer of barbed wire. The business behind it was a hodgepodge of broken-down cars, rusted washers and dryers, pipes, old furniture, and heaps of metal that no longer resembled anything. Two heavy-duty cranes loomed over the heaps, one with a magnet and one with a hungry-looking claw attachment. A weathered plywood sign told them that this was WOLFF'S SCRAPYARD.

She gestured at Sister Wanda, and the two of them put on their brakes.

"What should we do here?" Bicycle asked the Fortune.

It answered with a question mark.

They pushed the gate open and headed for a trailer that looked to be the scrapyard's office. A sign was mounted to the trailer's roof that said SMILE! YOU'RE ON OUR VIDEO SECU-RITY CAMERAS! Another one had a picture of a German shepherd and the words I CAN MAKE IT TO THE FENCE IN 2.8 SECONDS. CAN YOU? Sister Wanda left her bike at the bottom of the trailer's stairs. Bicycle carried the Fortune inside so it could hear what was said.

A man with a ponytail and bushy muttonchop whis-kers knelt in front of a filing cabinet. "Hey, folks," he said in a gravelly voice. He climbed to his feet and brushed at his grease-spotted coveralls. "Are you dropping that off for scrap? We'll need to get it weighed first."

"No!" Bicycle exclaimed, clasping the Fortune's top tube to her chest. "This isn't scrap!"

"Sorry. We had our bike event this week. I thought you might have been a latecomer."

Sister Wanda asked, "What bike event was that, Mr. . . . ?"

"Mr. Wolff, madam." He extended his hand to her. "We got in a shipment of old, broken-down bikes, some complete, some just frames. Don't know much about bikes myself, but sometimes still-usable stuff shows up. Even collector's items. So I decided to invite the public to come see if they'd like to purchase any before we processed them."

"Processed them?" Bicycle asked.

"You know, recycled them. We do it all here—we got the shears, the crusher, the chopper, the shredder, the grinder, and the baler to bind it all together." He nodded out the

33

trailer's window, where they could see another man operating the claw crane. The crane picked up one heap and dropped it into a gray compactor, which made a screechy grinding noise. A few sparks flew into the air. "We've got a crucible on order, too. That one's for melting."

Bicycle couldn't tell if the shiver she felt was hers or the Fortune's. "For melting?" she repeated. She'd have preferred living her whole life without knowing that some bikes ended up sheared, crushed, chopped, shredded, ground, baled, or melted.

Sister Wanda put a hand on Bicycle's shoulder and squeezed. "Actually, we are here to look at the bikes and frames. We'll take whatever wasn't already sold."

Bicycle looked at her guardian with gratitude. She could almost see the nun's brain busily calculating how they'd afford such a thing, plus how they'd ship the bikes back to the monastery.

"Sorry, ma'am. Everything's been processed. My son Chuck is baling the remains right now." He looked at Bicycle's stricken face. "Kid, the metal from those recycled bikes will get made into all kinds of new stuff. Heck, most of it probably ends up being used to make new bikes. Recycled cycles!" His rough chuckle rasped on Bicycle's ears. The office phone rang. "If there's nothing else I can do for you . . . ?" he asked, moving to pick up the call.

"No, nothing more, thank you, Mr. Wolff," said Sister Wanda.

Outside, Bicycle asked the Fortune, "Do you think that was what was pulling you here? Did you have a sixth sense that a bunch of bikes needed to be rescued?"

I have many more than six senses. If that is what happened, I should have been smart enough to get here sooner.

"Don't be too hard on yourself," Sister Wanda said. "Even the smartest among us isn't perfect. Although this is an unfortunate end to our trip, let us try to remember that recycling is meant to give old items a new life. What seems like an end can be viewed as a new beginning."

Bicycle closed her eyes and sent up a wish that most of the bikes had been bought, and that any recycled frames would have a speedy trip to a factory that would make them into new bikes for riders to buy and love. She opened her eyes and watched the crane operator pick up another load. "Can we get out of here?" she said.

"Indeed," said Sister Wanda. "Time to head for the Nearly Silent Nunnery."

Using the Fortune's map, they found the nunnery on a side street back near the heart of Harpers Ferry. The nuns welcomed them with hushed hospitality. Bicycle tried to engage her bike in conversation before bed, but it put her off with one-word answers. It played no music, yawped no alarms. The Fortune was dead silent all night long.

In the morning, Sister Wanda offered to help the nunnery manager with a few things. She suggested Bicycle take her bike outside for some air. The day was overcast and gray, barely a ray of sunlight to be found.

Bicycle asked the Fortune, "Do you want to go for a spin around the neighborhood?"

No.

Bicycle found a bench. "Do you want to sit with me under this tree?"

No.

She plopped herself on the bench and leaned the bike next to her. "I want to help you feel better, but I don't know how. What would cheer you up right now?"

I was not programmed to cheer up.

"I've seen you do a lot of things you weren't programmed to do," Bicycle said, impatience creeping into her voice. She took a deep breath. "I feel sad about what happened yesterday, too."

The Fortune blinked, What would cheer you up right now?

Bicycle waggled her head back and forth, thinking about it. She noticed a convenience store on the corner. "A candy bar." She'd had eggs and toast for breakfast, but some mornings are better faced with a chunk of chocolate.

I cannot eat candy bars. Could you eat one for me? If you cheer yourself up, it might cheer me up at the same time.

Bicycle liked this suggestion. She felt in her pocket to make sure she had some money on her. "How about this? I will bring the candy bar back here and describe every bite for you. Then you'll have more data. That's one of your favorite things."

Yes, it is, the Fortune agreed.

Bicycle walked to the corner and crossed at the traffic light. The store's array of candy choices turned out to be impressive. Bicycle surveyed the grand riches before her. Should she choose a treat that she knew she liked, or something she'd never heard of before? What was an Abba-Zabba? Or an Idaho Spud?

She reached for an intriguing candy bar called a Malty Melty from the display next to the checkout counter and the store clerk laughed.

"How long did it take you to eat the one you got over the weekend, less than a minute?" the clerk asked. "Maybe you'd better buy two this time."

"Excuse me?" Bicycle said. "I didn't buy one before. This is my first time here."

"Oh, I see." The clerk winked and nodded like she and Bicycle were sharing a secret. "Didn't buy one before. Got it."

Bicycle nodded back, because it seemed like the easiest thing to do. She plunked the Malty Melty bar on the counter along with some money.

The clerk counted out the change with agonizing slowness. She said, "You know, I bet I could learn to tell you apart because of what you buy. You, you're the Melty." She winked again. "See you some other time, I'm sure."

Bicycle thanked the clerk, whose odd behavior had reminded her that wherever one traveled, there were interesting people. She hurried out the door. Traffic had picked up, and she had to wait for several buses to pass. The sides of the buses identified them as free parking shuttles. Bicycle had learned last night that a big chunk of the town of Harpers Ferry was the site of a national historic park. The area had become famous when John Brown, an abolitionist, had tried to seize weapons from the local armory before the Civil War in order to free slaves in the area. Brown's revolt had failed, but his brave act inspired others who wanted slavery to end. Bicycle thought how some things were worth doing, no matter whether one succeeded or not.

Once she was back, she sat down and told the Fortune, "Okay, I've got one." She held up the Malty Melty's wrapper for her bike to scan. "I've never had this kind before, so this'll be new for both of us." She unpeeled it and chomped. She was unable to talk for a few chews and simply made *mmm*ing noises.

Would you say it is delicious? Scrumptious? Flavorsome? Delectable? Mouthwatering?

Bicycle swallowed. "It's yummy. The outside is a milk chocolate shell, and inside is a whipped chocolate filling. There's a different flavor in there, too." She took another bite.

Malt powder is on the ingredient list; perhaps that is the flavor. Is your mouth now cheerful? Does that make the rest of you cheerful?

"My mouth is a little drooly and my tongue is tingling." Bicycle kept munching and describing, trying not to talk with her mouth full, as Sister Wanda had taught her. Focusing on the sensations of eating made eating even more satisfying. She'd have to try eating some of her other favorite foods "for" the Fortune.

She realized she was down to the last bite and glanced toward the convenience store, considering going back for another one.

She left her mouth open midchew. If Sister Wanda had been there, she'd have asked Bicycle if she'd been born in a barn.

A girl. Seated on the bus stop bench across the street. Identical-looking to Bicycle, except she was wearing a pair of cargo shorts and a T-shirt covered in pockets. Identical hair, identical face, identical body shape. She also held a Malty Melty in her hand poised between one bite and the next.

They gaped at each other.

A moment later, Bicycle's jaw dropped even lower. Sister Wanda would have had a conniption fit at the way she was showing her malted-goo-coated tongue to the whole world. Bicycle's shock came from seeing *another* mirror image of her own familiar self strolling up behind her seated doppelgänger.

This new person also held a candy bar, but one with a blue-and-white wrapper. She stopped short and joined in the stare.

Bicycle's mind started chattering unhelpfully, trying to remember the name of the candy bar this other girl was holding. *It's called Almond something. Almond Surprise? Almond Crunch? I bet the Fortune will know. I'll ask it that after I ask it what the odds are that three people could look so similar.*

Two more girls came out of the convenience store, playfully trying to steal each other's candy bars. If Bicycle hadn't known that neither of these girls was her, she wouldn't have been able to tell. She thought her chin might drop to her chest and drizzle her shirt with chocolate.

Once the two clowning girls noticed the first two staring, they also turned to look at Bicycle. A thousand seconds passed.

One of them said, "That's her, isn't it?"

Another answered, "Who else could it be?"

Their voices carried distinctly across the morning air.

A woman with the thickest glasses Bicycle had ever seen emerged from the convenience store with a granola bar. She had unruly black hair barely held back from her face by a toothed clip. She noticed the frozen tableau of girls and squinted across the street, shading her eyes with one hand. She asked, "What's everyone staring at?"

"Yoof!" the doppelgänger on the bench called out to Bicycle. She jumped up and began waving her candy bar. "It's us!"

YOOF!

A bus pulled up to the bus stop and momentarily blocked Bicycle's view of the girls and the woman. She thought she could hear excited yelling over the bus engine's grumble. When it pulled away, the group ran across the street and pulled Bicycle off the bench into a giant jumping group hug. Bicycle felt the woman's arms hugging the tightest. She heard five voices repeating, "It's us!" and "It's you!" and that mysterious syllable "Yoof!" over and over. She was too astonished to do anything more than let the hug happen.

The woman turned her head and yelled, "Alex? Where is your father? Alex!" After a minute, Bicycle heard a man's voice ask what all the hugging was about.

"Count the girls, Alex!" the woman said, and started sobbing.

The man counted out loud, "One, two, three, four, . . . *five?*

Yoof? Yoof! How? Really? Let me in there!" Two more arms joined in the hug clump.

Then a familiar voice cut through the babble and the *yoof*ing. "Excuse me!" Sister Wanda had arrived. "Bicycle, are you in there somewhere? Please unhand my girl!" Bicycle managed to unwind herself and get behind the nun.

"*Your* girl? She's *ours*. We've finally found her!" announced the woman. Wayward tendrils of her uptwisted hair were escaping everywhere, some sticking to her face.

"What are you . . . talking . . . abou . . . ?" Sister Wanda trailed off without even finishing the last word of her question. She'd gotten a good look at the four new girls who'd been part of the hugging scrum. Sister Wanda seemed to be caught up in her own born-in-a-barn gaping stare. Then her manners took over, and she managed to close her mouth. She began quietly repeating, "Oh my. My oh my oh my."

"We're her identical sisters," said the girl with all the pockets. "Quintuplets, since there's five of us altogether."

Bicycle could see the half-eaten Malty Melty bar poking out of her cargo shorts.

The woman said, "We've been looking for her for years. Years! And here she is, right in front of us." She wiped ineffectually at her hair-plastered cheeks and grabbed Bicycle again, crushing her in a hug that felt like it had indeed been years in coming.

Bicycle woofed out a short, heavy breath. Like anyone who'd inexplicably turned up without any explanation on some steps as a young child, she'd wondered if she'd ever find her birth family. Should she start sobbing, too, overjoyed at being found after so long? Instead, she felt sort of numb. And a bit squished.

"We never gave up hope," said the man.

Bicycle took a good look at him. Short dark-blond hair, bushy-ish eyebrows, round face. She couldn't tell if he was familiar at all. He looked nice, though. And stunned.

"Have you been here in Harpers Ferry the whole time?" he asked Bicycle.

"No," Bicycle said. "I came here because my bike—" She stopped. How could she even begin to explain why she was here? "Have *you* been here in Harpers Ferry the whole time?" she asked back.

He said, "No, we just moved here this month. Our new home is near the parking area where shuttle buses bring tourists to the historic section of town. We caught one of them today to get a few treats, because some mornings are better faced with a chunk of chocolate." Bicycle made a surprised little sound, which he misinterpreted. "Right, why am I talking about chocolate? It doesn't matter. I bet you have oodles of questions, and we do, too. We should go back home and ask our oodles until we're done."

"Yes," agreed the woman.

The woman—*My mom?* Bicycle suddenly thought—released her. Bicycle looked up into her face. Warm brown eyes swam behind bottle-thick glasses. Did she know those eyes?

Sister Wanda, flustered, said, "Hold on, before we go anywhere, I'd like some proof that you are who you say you are."

The woman said, "You must be looking out for our girl here, and I appreciate that, but there's no need to protect her from us, of all people. Look at her! And them!" She swept her hands in front of the four girls standing together. She said, "Really look at them! If you didn't already know which one was which, would you know?"

Bicycle clenched a hand, wanting Sister Wanda to glance at the group and say in her no-nonsense tone, *Of course I would, I'd know my Bicycle anywhere.*

Instead, the nun studied the five faces in silence. She blinked an excessive number of times. "We certainly do have a lot of questions that need answering." She looked over her shoulder at the Nearly Silent Nunnery. The sight of the place seemed to steady her. "Please humor me. Let's go in there to talk first. I'm certain they can find a space for us." She started up the sidewalk as if sure everyone would follow her. Everyone did.

As they walked over, one of the girls said, "I guess we should introduce ourselves. I'm Apple." She was holding a Twix bar.

Bicycle hoped they wouldn't eat their candy bars or put them down too soon, because it seemed like a good way to keep track of who was who. She then realized she'd somehow lost the last bite of her own Malty Melty in the crazy hug.

"Apple's the smart one. I'm the one who doesn't look before I leap," said the next girl, the one with the candy bar in the blue-and-white wrapper. *Almond Joy—that was the name of that bar,* Bicycle's mind chattered. If only her other questions could be answered so easily.

"We're equally smart," argued Apple. "I just happen to work hardest on my homeschool assignments." She told Bicycle, "The name of this leaping-before-looking person is—sort of—Banana. Sometimes, though, she's called anything but Banana. Do you have a different name today?"

Anything-but-Banana said with a regal air, "Today I would prefer to be called Bernice. Now allow me to introduce your sister Cookie, the girl covered in way too many pockets."

"I like pockets! I sew extra ones on all my clothes. And I like my name, not like Banan—er, Bernice," said Cookie. "I think my name makes me sound friendly, which I am. Our sister behind the camera lens is Daphne, who goes by Daff."

Bicycle turned to check what Daff's candy bar was (a Kit

Kat) and saw Daff had whipped out a small camera as they entered the nunnery. Daff said, "This is how the reunion began. Say hi for posterity, Yoof."

Bicycle waved awkwardly at the camera. "Hi."

In the foyer, Sister Wanda said a few words to the nun who silently greeted them. They were then ushered into the empty dining hall.

Before they sat down, the woman—*Mom?* Bicycle tried out the name again when she looked at her—stuck her hand out for Sister Wanda to shake. "We adults should introduce ourselves. I'm Stella Kosroy, and this is my husband, Alex. Wait, what am I doing? If you've been taking care of our girl all this time, you're practically family!" She yanked on Sister Wanda's hand to pull her in for a hug.

"Oof—well, yes, I suppose that's so. I'm Sister Wanda Magdalena. I've been your daughter's guardian since she turned up on my doorstep when she was no more than a toddler. Please, sit." They all did so. Bicycle parked the Fortune at the end of the table.

Alex Kosroy—*Dad?* Bicycle thought—said, "We've been missing our daughter Euphemia here for nearly nine years."

"What did you call me?" Bicycle asked.

"Oh yeah, we've got to explain the names, Mom," said Daff. "In fact, let me get it on video."

"Who should start the story?" said Bernice-Banana.

Bicycle wondered how often she changed her name.

"Me, because I'm the firstborn," said Apple.

"How about Mom, because she was there for all of it, even before we were born," said Cookie.

"Dad was, too," said Apple.

"We all know the story backward and forward. Any of us could tell it," said Bernice-Banana.

Daff leaned in. "All right, a historical family film moment, captured by Daff Kosroy. Here's Euphemia, back from wherever she's been. She's about to learn the story of her name, because she's never heard it before."

"Once upon a time, twelve long years ago," began Apple, "Mom gave birth to five perfect identical quintuplet girls. And even though she'd known for months she was going to give birth to these quintuplet girls, she and Dad had not planned out names for any of them."

Mom took over. "Because I believed since the universe had given us such a special and unexpected gift, the universe would step in and tell me your names when it was time for me to know them."

Bicycle saw the Fortune's screen blink: Less than one in fifty-five million births are quintuplets.

Bernice-Banana began talking next. "Apparently, the universe was feeling bonkers, because when the nurse came over to Mom to ask her for our names, she said—"

Dad jumped in, "In this deep, resounding voice, not like her normal voice at all—"

Bernice-Banana continued, "In this deep, the-universe-is-speaking voice, Mom said our names were Apple, Banana, Cookie, Daphne, and Euphemia."

Cookie said, "Dad asked her if she was sure about all of the names, if she didn't want to think about it a little bit, since these were quite uncommon names, especially if you think about them as a group, and she should remember that their daughters would carry them through their whole lives. I'm glad what Mom said next was—"

"THE UNIVERSE HAS SPOKEN," Daff said, turning the camera on herself. "Dad said he'd never seen Mom look like that, or talk like that, before or since. He said any woman who had just given birth to quintuplets should have the right to name them whatever she wanted."

Bicycle kept turning this way and that to follow what they were saying. It was as if the Kosroys were tossing a conversational ball back and forth between them.

Apple took up the story next. "We personally can't help but think the alphabet wallpaper in our old nursery may have had some effect on Mom's mind, since it had 'A is for Apple, B is for Banana, C is for Cookie' repeated around the room."

"If the alphabet wallpaper had that much power over me, then why didn't I name Daphne 'Drumstick' and Euphemia 'Egg'?" asked their mother.

Bernice-Banana jumped in. "Because even someone

hypnotized by wallpaper knows deep down that naming a child 'Drumstick' or 'Egg' would be . . . bananas."

Daff said, "You told us you read every Scooby-Doo comic book in Dad's vintage collection on sleepless nights when you were pregnant. That had an effect on your mind, too, and inspired you to name me after the brave and well-dressed teen detective Daphne Blake."

Their mother shook her head. "I'm telling you, the universe spoke through me. The name Euphemia didn't come from any wallpaper or comic book. None of you have ever been able to explain the origin of Euphemia's name."

Sister Wanda murmured to Bicycle, "You know, Saint Euphemia was the founder of my order of nuns. Maybe the universe knew you would end up with one of us."

"I'm Euphemia Kosroy?" said Bicycle, trying it on to see if it seemed familiar. It actually felt like a much-too-large hat.

"Don't worry, you've got a nickname," said Cookie. "Yoof."

Bicycle puzzled it out for a minute and realized that the first syllable of "Euphemia"—"Euph"—was pronounced "Yoof." She said, "I think I'd like to stick with the name I've had for as long as I can remember: Bicycle." She was still a little dizzy from following the conversation that had jumped back and forth among the Kosroys, and she definitely didn't want to agree to anything as major as a new name or nickname right now.

"Ooh!" said Bernice-Banana. "That's a good one! Mom, why couldn't you have bought nursery wallpaper that said 'B is for Bicycle'?" She directed her next question at Bicycle. "Can I trade names with you?"

"Oh . . . no, thanks," said Bicycle.

"No one wants to be a Banana," sighed Bernice-Banana.

Sister Wanda seized control of the conversation's bouncing ball. "So how did you lose your fifth child? How did she end up on our steps in Washington, D.C.?"

Dad said, "D.C.? This is the first time we've known for sure what city she ended up in." He and Mom looked at each other, pain in their eyes.

Mom said, "The police were searching, the FBI was searching, everyone was searching everywhere as soon as we realized Yoof was missing. We're not wealthy people, but we also hired private investigators over the years to try to piece it together. We never once stopped looking." She briefly pressed her hands to her lips. "A big part of the problem was that we weren't sure when you disappeared. There were so many possibilities to chase down."

"We've been telling Mom and Dad the whole time that you were okay," said Apple. "I bet you've heard of identical twins sharing each other's emotions. Well, we've got that times five, so all of us know when any one of us is hurt." She tipped her thumb at Bernice-Banana. "I knew the minute she tripped and scraped her arm yesterday. So while everyone's been looking for you, we've known beyond a doubt that, somewhere, you were safe and pretty happy. It's been awful not having you with us, but at least we knew that much."

"Do you remember us?" asked Mom.

"What's your Quint Sense been telling you?" asked Bernice-Banana. "Was it letting you know your big ol' family was somewhere that you weren't?"

The Kosroys locked six pairs of eyes on Bicycle while she tried to organize her thoughts. When she was young, she'd sometimes imagined that she was a lost princess and would be found by her royal relatives coming to the doorstep in a horse-drawn carriage. As she'd gotten older, she'd sometimes dreamed that she might be related to different famous bike racers. But in all the times she'd imagined her family finding her, had they looked anything like this? She had to be honest.

"I'm sorry," she said. "But no. I don't remember anything about you."

SOFT HIDING PLACES

Bicycle thought her statement might silence the group, but everyone started talking at once, including Sister Wanda. Bicycle couldn't make heads or tails out of any of it, so she just watched them. She used the opportunity to commit to memory that Cookie was the pocket girl, Daff was the one with the camera, Bernice-Banana had a scraped elbow, and Apple had an aura of confidence about her, like she could come up with an answer for anything.

Sister Wanda raised her voice until no one else had any choice but to listen to her. "You mentioned before you didn't know when Bicycle disappeared. What did you mean by that?"

Their mom's eyes welled up with tears again. "I want to make sure you know how much I love you," she said to Bicycle. "I love all my girls the same. I never meant for this to happen. I—we—just needed so much help."

Sister Wanda softened her tone and said, "I'm sure this has been very hard for you."

Mom wiped a finger under each side of her glasses and nodded. "It's been a nightmare. And it happened partly because we *got* all the help we needed, and then some."

"When the girls started to walk," said Dad, "it became clear that two people raising them was never going to be enough. But I edit math textbooks and Stella writes crossword puzzles, so there was no way we could afford day care or nannies. Then we got lucky. We were invited to live at Worldwide Twintopia in Paramus, New Jersey."

"Not the best name for a place that also has families of triplets, quadruplets, and quints," said Apple.

"Better than its original name, though: the Worldwide Global Goods MegaMall! Deals Too Big for Just One Continent," said Bernice-Banana in a voice like a television game show host. "We lived with a whole bunch of other families with multiples—you know, two or more children born at the same time—in this mall that got converted into a commune."

"Commune?" asked Bicycle, unsure of what the word meant.

Mom explained. "A cooperative community, where we share everything. We share the work, we share expenses, and we help take care of each other. The owner was a twin himself, and he knew it can be hard for parents to raise multiples. When his mall property wasn't showing a profit, he decided to convert the stores into apartments for families with twins or more who were struggling to find enough money or time or both to take care of their kids. He made the food court into a big shared dining hall and meeting room. He turned the mall office space into a giant day care with an attached doctor's office. We were so lucky to be able to move in. Except . . ."

Dad said, "Except we had one daughter who loved to roam her new home." He smiled at Bicycle. "You'd climb into other kids' cribs in the big nursery when you wanted someone to play with; you'd wander into other people's homes and take naps; you'd join other families' tables during lunch or dinner. You never had a fear of strangers. You thought everyone was there to welcome you. But that's the thing about Twintopia—that's how it's supposed to be! All us parents were outnumbered, we needed more loving, helping hands to keep our children safe, so every one of us pitched in when *anyone's* kids needed attention."

Mom's eyes were streaming. "That's why we weren't sure when you went missing. You were often off somewhere else, napping, snacking, playing. Both Alex and I were sleeping very strange hours. Even with support, we were still blearily beyond exhaustion. Our girls' schedules were all over the map, and often they'd sleep in the big nursery. I was so grateful for the help, I stopped being vigilant for a little while. I stopped doing the best job keeping track of everyone. I didn't count my girls every day." Her voice got hoarse. "We think it could have been a week before we realized our Yoof was gone."

Apple, Bernice-Banana, Cookie, and Daff moved at the same time, but Cookie made it to Mom first to give her a hug. Bicycle wanted to help comfort her, too, somehow. At least she knew now that she'd been misplaced, not intentionally given away.

A tiny memory poked up its nose from the ocean of her early childhood. "Did I go looking for nooks, corners, places I could hide?"

"Laundry baskets!" said her mother, laughing through fresh tears. "Baskets full of clean laundry were your favorite, but you'd also burrow into closets and pull down winter coats to make a nest, or climb into dry bathtubs with a bunch of towels. You loved small, soft places."

"When Bicycle appeared on our doorstep, I guessed she was about three years old," said Sister Wanda. "How close was I?"

"She went missing right before their third birthday," Dad said. "We wanted to get them together for a group photo, and we were able to round up all the girls except Yoof. We searched the whole place, up and down. It was just after we'd had weeks of visitors arriving at Twintopia: deliveries, donations coming in, plus these moviemakers who were doing a documentary on families of multiples. That was the worst day of our lives." Dad rubbed his eyes with one hand while Mom clasped his other. "We still don't know what happened. We think Yoof found a cozy spot in one of the delivery boxes. We'd had shipments of pillows, couches, bread, clothes—so many piles of soft stuff—and someone drove off with her by accident to their next delivery location. We called the delivery companies, but no one had seen Yoof. The FBI, police, and private investigators tried to trace the deliveries, but didn't come up with anything. I can't imagine how she made it from New Jersey to Washington, D.C."

"Did she talk to you?" Mom asked Sister Wanda. "When you found her? She was a late bloomer when it came to talking, so we worried that she couldn't tell someone her name."

"It took some doing to get her to speak to me," admitted Sister Wanda.

"We always spoke for Yoof," said Apple.

"Yeah, she didn't have to talk because we knew what she wanted and would help her get it," said Cookie.

"We knew her favorite foods, her favorite stuffed animals," said Bernice-Banana.

"Her favorite clothes, her favorite books," added Daff.

"We've always known everything about each other," finished Apple.

After having watched the six members of her family volley their sentences back and forth, Bicycle wasn't surprised that she hadn't spoken as a child. She may have been trying to interject some silence into the conversations.

"Now you know all we know," said Dad. "Maybe you can tell us what life has been like on your end, Yoof—that is, Bicycle. Can you start with your name?"

Sister Wanda and Bicycle did their best to explain how she'd shown up on the steps of the Mostly Silent Monastery and all the adventures she'd had since. No one remembered the pink BICYCLE T-shirt she'd been wearing the day she was found— they thought maybe she'd borrowed it from another family's laundry basket. Everyone laughed to learn that pink shirt was the reason Sister Wanda began calling her Bicycle. They agreed that while they'd never know exactly how Bicycle had ended up at the monastery, everyone was thankful she did. Lunchtime loomed when they'd finished covering the basics.

The nuns offered the group plates of sandwiches and potato chips. The Kosroys kept chatting away, not seeming to notice that they were the only table in the dining room using more than eight words. Stella and Alex explained to Sister Wanda that the maintenance on the old Twintopia Mall property had become too expensive, so the commune had picked up and moved into an empty school building here in West Virginia. Dad said, "Our new apartment is a former classroom, but it works for us. Most days, we homeschool the girls in the mornings and get our work done in the afternoons." He turned to Bicycle and said, "Just think, tonight you'll be sleeping in your own bunk bed with your sisters!"

Bicycle lost her grip on a chip. "Oh," she said. It hadn't occurred to her that she was meant to go live with these people. There was no doubt in her mind that this was her birth family and that the story they'd told was true. But did going home with them mean she'd never return to the monastery? Was she supposed to change her life completely in no time flat?

Sister Wanda appeared to have heard every bit of Bicycle's anxiety inside the word "Oh." The nun said, "We are so happy to have found you, but surely you understand that this will be a big adjustment for Bicycle. Perhaps it would make the most sense for her to stay the night with you but then return to the monastery with me to pack and prepare for her move."

"Out of the question," Mom said. "I'm never letting Bicycle out of my sight again."

"You'd be very welcome to come to the monastery with us," Sister Wanda said.

"That'd pose a bit of a problem," Dad said. "All the families share one car at Twintopia, and our turn to drive it won't come up for several more weeks."

"I see," Sister Wanda said. She cleared her throat. "Then I propose this: I will go with you to Twintopia to see Bicycle settled in, and when I return to the monastery, I will mail her belongings. As soon as you are able, I would be most grateful if you could bring Bicycle to the monastery. She has many people there who love her and will want to wish her well in this next chapter in her life." She put an arm around Bicycle and said in a low voice, "I've had you for so long, it wouldn't be fair not to share you with your family. It's the right thing to do."

So. Bicycle's life *was* changing completely in no time flat. She felt as if a river had suddenly burst out of the ground before her and was sweeping her away in its current. Sister Wanda and her parents were telling her not to swim against it, or try to get back to dry land, but to let it take her where it would. She hoped this wasn't what sisterhood and daughter-hood would permanently feel like.

The swept-away-by-the-current feeling accompanied Bicycle while she and Sister Wanda loaded their bikes onto the front-mounted rack of a shuttle bus and climbed aboard with the Kosroys. As the bus wheezed up a hill, her mother peppered her with questions about her habits and her favorite things. She then turned her attention to Bicycle's recent cross-country trip. "How on earth did Sister Wanda agree to you riding across country by yourself?" Her mother shivered. "I can't bear to think of what might have happened!"

"I didn't exactly get a chance to agree to that plan," Sister Wanda said drily. "Rather than attend a friendship-making camp in which I'd enrolled her, Bicycle set out by herself to make her own friends on her bike ride."

Mom's questions continued as they disembarked from the bus and walked across a parking lot, up a street, and down a half-circle driveway surrounded by overgrown grass.

Bicycle noticed the Fortune blinking, Please ask your mother how literally she meant her statement about never letting you out of her sight again. Will she choose not to sleep? Will she follow you at all times while asking questions?

Bicycle figured she'd find out soon enough. They arrived at the front double doors of a sprawling brick building. The block letters glued to the bricks announced it was the Jefferson County Junior-Senior Regional High School. In one window someone with very neat handwriting had taped up a piece of paper that said WELCOME TO TWINTOPIA!

Dad waved at the paper and said, "There's still a lot of work to do, like getting a new sign made and mowing the playing fields, but we had to get the inside set up first." He unlocked the door and held it open with a grin. "Come and see your home sweet home."

A SISTER FOUR TIMES OVER

"I'll lead the tour," said Bernice-Banana, turning to walk backward and pointing in different directions down the locker-lined hallways. "The shared nursery where all the littlest littles go is in the gym. The band rehearsal room is the shared playroom. The cafeteria's where we have common meals. There's fifty families here, so around three hundred people total."

Bicycle wondered where everyone could be. The hallways were so quiet, it reminded her of the Mostly Silent Monastery, where there were at most sixty monks at any given time. But then Bernice-Banana said, "This is the afternoon lull—lots of the littles nap now, and there's always a group activity in the playroom, like storytime, book club, family yoga, sing-alongs, or this thing called Crafternoon that's a free-for-all with paper, glue, markers, cardboard boxes, and glitter."

Each classroom door had a narrow vertical window; a piece of construction paper with a last name on it, like MARTIN or SOWSIAN or FALALU; and a welcome mat in front of it. Some of the doors were decorated for the season with witches on broomsticks or Indian corn bundles, and a few families had put out jack-o'-lanterns. Each hallway looked like a miniature neighborhood.

Bicycle followed her family through so many sets of doors and turned so many corners that she lost track. She murmured to the Fortune, "Can you make a map of this place?"

I am already doing so.

"You'll always be able to find our apartment by following the states," Apple told Bicycle. She pointed at the floor, where Bicycle's sneakers scuffed across a yellow painting of Louisiana with a star labeled BATON ROUGE. "They're in alphabetical order and lead in a loop starting from the cafeteria. The students who used to attend this school did it as an art project using special paint that won't wear off for a hundred years or something. We live next to Missouri."

Bernice-Banana said, "I feel a song coming on." She threw her arms wide and chanted the opening words to the song "Fifty Nifty United States."

"Alabama, Alaska, Arizona, Arkansas," Cookie took up the tune.

"California, Colorado, Connecticut," Daff chimed in. She clapped twice. "Take it, Yoof!" She looked at Bicycle.

Were there more C states or was D next? Bicycle thought. The Fortune saved her by playing a chorus of kids' voices singing, "Delaware, Florida, Georgia, Hawaii, Idaho."

"What a neat trick," Cookie said. "Can your bike play other songs, too?" The Fortune responded by playing the Sesame Street song "C Is for Cookie." The family laughed.

"My bike is pretty special," Bicycle told them. "It has tons of features, and uses this computer screen to communicate by writing out words."

"A bike that can write? Who can keep up with technology today?" asked Mom, shaking her head in disbelief.

"If I had a bike like that, I might be convinced that we need to learn to ride," Apple said.

"You don't know how to ride a bike?" Bicycle asked, looking at Apple and then the rest of her family. "Any of you?"

Dad said, "I learned as a kid, but I haven't done it in years."

"I never learned to ride or drive," said Mom. "I'm as near-sighted as a rhinoceros, which is about as near-sighted as it gets."

Before Bicycle could absorb these facts, Mom stopped and bent over to unlock a classroom door. Seven tissue-paper ghosts made a frame around the construction-paper label THE KOSROYS.

"Here we are. Please excuse the mess."

The classroom was divided in half by a thick green-and-blue-striped curtain that reminded Bicycle of a circus big top. The half of the room where they now stood was crowded with furniture. It had three couches pushed together to make a U-shape around a braided rug. One wall had several jam-packed bookcases and two tall cabinets standing against a blackboard. In the far corner near the windows was a kitchenette with a sink, a mini fridge, a microwave, and a table and chairs. Near the curtain sat a cubbyhole desk piled with papers and pens, and a piano topped by a leaning stack of music books.

A tall basket filled with jumbled pairs of shoes sat next to the door. Every available space on the walls had been covered with hooks from which hung coats, bags, and droopy-fronded spider plants. Things were messy, but in an agreeable way that invited you to make yourself comfortable.

"I believe in having a place for everything and everything in its place, but it's a smaller space than we used to have," Mom said, fluttering her hands like she wanted to tidy the whole apartment at once. She scooped a blanket off the rug and draped it on the back of a couch.

"It's charming," said Sister Wanda. "I assume the bedrooms are behind that curtain?"

"Exactly," Dad said. "Girls, can you show your sister and Sister Wanda your room?" He tugged his wife away from arranging couch pillows toward the mini fridge. "We'll be there in a minute."

"Park your bike here," Apple suggested. "Our bedroom doesn't have much space to spare."

Bicycle patted the Fortune's handlebars. "I'll be right back," she told it.

I'll be right here, blinked the Fortune.

Apple wasn't kidding about the lack of spare space. Four chests of drawers spewing clothes surrounded a set of regular bunk beds and a set of triple bunk beds. Hooks were hung with stuffed animals, including a serenely smiling sloth. The braided rug in here was covered by piles of DVDs and notebooks, a robotics kit, and a box of modeling clay. Three wardrobes had been set up to create a divider between the girls' bedroom and that of their parents.

Cookie hurriedly moved a stack of books off the bottom bed of the triple bunk and added them to a pile on the floor. She smoothed the coverlet. "This one's yours. It's clean. We always make your bed with fresh sheets the same time we make ours. Mom made it part of our routine. I guess she wanted to be ready for you coming back."

"Where's Yoof's pillow?" Bernice-Banana asked, scanning the other beds. "Ha-ha, Apple, you thief. How come you didn't foretell Yoof coming home with your all-seeing eye and leave her bed alone?" Bernice-Banana handed

Bicycle her missing pillow and said, "Apple's got the most mind-reading power. It can be pretty annoying."

"I do not have an all-seeing eye," Apple said. "I can just feel what's going on with my sisters. Which, you should know, can be pretty annoying in its own way." She explained to Bicycle, "Quint Sense is not like mind-reading. If we continually absorbed one another's thoughts and feelings, our brains would be chaotic messes. A feeling has to be big for us to pick up on it, or we have to focus really hard." She cocked her head. "You really don't remember us?" Her brown eyes were penetrating.

Bicycle shook her head. Dad called out from the other side of the room, "We've got a surprise, c'mon back over here!"

Once she parted the curtain, Mom and Dad started singing to her, "Welcome home to you! Welcome home to you! Welcome home, dear Euphemia-now-Bicycle! Welcome home to you!"

Daphne took out her camera. Dad held up a frozen cheesecake from which a porcupine's worth of lit candles bristled. "This is all the candles we have in the house. It'll have to represent all the birthdays we've missed with you."

"If you had enough candles to cover every birthday she's missed with our family, it'd be three plus four plus five plus six plus seven plus eight plus nine plus ten plus eleven plus twelve, so seventy-five total," said Apple. "Hey, I bet you don't know when your—our—birthday is."

Bicycle shook her head again.

"It's November twenty-ninth, which is easy to remember because eleven and twenty-nine are both prime numbers."

Dad said, "Sorry, we can't eat the cheesecake quite yet because it just came out of the freezer. Whoo! Hold on." He put it down on the table. "Got a little toasty there. Maybe the candle flames will defrost it faster. Anyway, come over and make a wish."

"Make ten wishes!" said her mom, clasping her hands together.

Bicycle approached the blaze with a lot of thoughts, but no single clear wish, let alone ten of them. She looked at her mother and father, and thought with her first puff: *I have parents.* She looked at Apple, Bernice-Banana, Cookie, and Daff, and thought with the second puff: *I'm a sister four times over.* She looked at Sister Wanda with the third puff: *Do I really belong here?* The fourth through the ninth puffs: *Please let me figure this out.* The final puff: *Please.*

Everyone cheered.

It turned out that the candles did speed up defrosting. After the cake was consumed, Sister Wanda thanked the Kosroys for their hospitality but said she had to be going and push her pedals hard if she was going to make it home before dark. "I haven't raced the sunset in years, but it's what my body wants to do today."

Bicycle walked stiffly to the door with the nun, regretting that she hadn't used her candle wishes to make Sister Wanda stay the night. And the day after that. And maybe for another couple of months, you know, until she got the hang of living here.

They walked into the hallway for a moment of privacy.

Bicycle cut right to the chase. "How am I supposed to do this? Am I supposed to apply my friend-making rules to reuniting with family?" *But this was so different,* she thought. *Family you didn't have a choice about. They were yours and you were theirs whether you got along or not.*

Sister Wanda touched Bicycle's cheek. "Open your heart to them. They clearly have been longing for your return, and I am certain they will take good care of you."

"How do I open my heart?"

"What have the monks and I been teaching you your entire life? You start by listening." Sister Wanda wrapped her arms around Bicycle. The familiar smell of lilac soap enveloped her. It was much different from being enthusiastically squeezed by people who felt like strangers. "The Mostly Silent Monastery will always be your home, too.

We'll have you back soon for a nice long visit. I promise." She then released Bicycle and looked up at the ceiling, blinking rapidly. "I must go. I will call you every day."

She strode off. Bicycle knew that a piece of her heart, open or not, went with her.

The Kosroys' door opened so quickly that Bicycle suspected someone had been peeking through the curtain in the window.

"Come on back in, we want to show you the photo albums!" said Mom.

WHAT ANIMAL WOULD YOU BE?

Bicycle looked at pictures of herself as a pink, squinch-faced newborn. *How did they tell us apart?* she wondered with each new photograph of five babies in a crib, five babies sucking thumbs, five babies on a quilt. She tried to take Sister Wanda's advice and practice her listening skills. Instead, she had to answer a hundred more questions about herself and her life up until now.

Mom began asking how one addressed monks at the monastery but abruptly interrupted herself. "Oh my goodness. Does it feel difficult for you to call us Mom and Dad? Since you don't remember us? How can we make it easy for you? I mean, you don't have to say it until you are comfortable, but how can you get comfortable if you don't say it?"

Dad said, "Hey, that's a good point. Maybe you could start by calling us Alex and Stella—no, scratch that, that's too weird for me."

Before this, Bicycle had been thinking she'd try addressing them as Mom and Dad and see how it went—maybe it'd be like donning a much-too-large, my-name-is-Euphemia-sized hat and maybe it wouldn't—but now she was put on the spot and wasn't sure what to do.

Bernice-Banana held up her hands. "Here, I'll teach you. You pronounce them like this: Mo-om, Da-ad!" She stretched out the words with a groan in the middle.

This made everyone laugh, and before she could over-think it, Bicycle let the words tumble out. "Mom and Dad, Dad and Mom. I think it won't be a problem, but I'll let you know if it is." *Whew. No wrong-hat sensation at all,* she thought. Since she'd never called anyone those names before, it felt like using any new names for any new people in her life. Her parents both beamed at her, then launched into their next hundred questions.

That evening, the family headed to dinner in the cafeteria with the rest of Twintopia. Mom explained that everyone was on their own for breakfast, but when it was their turn, four families joined together to prepare lunch or dinner—gigantic meals that fed everyone. This wasn't an unfamiliar idea to Bicycle, since the Mostly Silent Monks also rotated kitchen duty, making big vats of stew, massive pans of casseroles, and towers of pancakes on breakfast-for-dinner night.

Maybe fitting in here will be a little easier because I'm used to living with lots of people already, she told herself.

However, as she followed her family through the now-crowded halls, she knew this was a whole new world. Families were chatting and kids were running in all directions to greet one another. A few rode scooters or pulled stuffed animals in wagons. Some girls were banging locker doors open and shut, and some boys were jumping rope and chanting about Miss Lucy and the lady with the alligator purse. Bicycle couldn't remember seeing more than a handful of monks in the monastery hallway at any one time. And they barely said anything. And they never jumped rope.

Dad showed Bicycle the communal chore wheel mounted on a bulletin board near the former principal's office. The wheel was nearly as big as the one on the television game show *Wheel of Fortune* and listed twenty-five different chores, like BATHROOM CLEANING and GROCERY SHOPPING. Index cards with families' last names and phone numbers were push-pinned to the bulletin board to show whose turn it was to do what. Again, this concept of sharing work was pretty familiar to Bicycle from the monastery. Some of the tasks weren't familiar, though, like NURSERY SHIFT and PLAYTIME REFEREES. She saw the Kosroy family's name next to something called QUAD DUTY.

A whiteboard outside the cafeteria this evening informed

the diners that they'd be enjoying borscht and black bean flautas. Bicycle had had borscht before—it was a thick beet soup mixed with sour cream. The flautas turned out to be crispy flute-shaped bean burritos with melted cheese on top. Bicycle had hardly bitten into her first one—*Yum,* she thought, *at least the weirdest day of my life has good food in it*—when she was interrupted by a group coming over to welcome her to the commune. After that, news of her arrival spread like wildfire through the cafeteria. Getting introduced to so many people one after another made her head spin with that carried-away-by-the-current feeling again.

Once bedtime approached, Bicycle was ready to conk out. She borrowed pajamas from Daff and fought to keep her eyes open through toothbrushing in the shared bathroom down the hall and a thorough tucking-in from Mom and Dad. Once the lights were out, though, it became apparent that her sisters weren't quite as ready for sleep as she was.

"Psst!" a sister said in the darkness above Bicycle's head. "Who's hungry still? I saved half of my Malty Melty in case." This had to be Cookie. Cookie, Daff, and Bicycle shared the triple-decker beds, with Bicycle on the bottom. Apple and Bernice-Banana shared the double bunk beds with Apple on top.

"Give it to Yoof," said someone else. "Sorry—I mean, give it to Bicycle. I promise we'll work on remembering your name."

Cookie's shadowy figure climbed down the bunk bed ladder and bent over Bicycle, whispering, "Maybe we'll call you Yoofcycle for a while."

Bicycle heard a crinkle and felt half a candy bar being pressed against her arm.

"Thanks," she said, putting it to the side of her pillow for tomorrow. Her bed shook gently as Cookie climbed back to the top.

"I bet you still have a ton of questions, like whether we have identical personalities." That came from Apple's direction. "We don't. It's kind of like we were all given an identical set of paints, but we each choose to paint different things with them."

"Speaking of paint, I bet you want to know if we all have the same favorite color. We do—it used to be pink and now it's orange." That was definitely Daff, because her voice came from the middle bunk over Bicycle's head.

"We don't all have the same favorite food, though. I hate to admit it, but mine is bananas. They're a terrific fruit, even if they're a terrible name." And that was Bernice-Banana. "What's yours?"

Bicycle yawned hugely. "I pretty much like food as a general rule."

Daff said in an undertone, "*We lay in the darkness, catching up on lost years, when she told us she liked food as a general rule.* Sorry—that sounded weird. When I want to remember something, sometimes I tell myself a story about it."

Bernice-Banana went on. "Cookie's favorite food is anything that she thinks smells good. Apple's crazy about noodles. Daff's our pizza gourmet."

"Hush, guys." That came from the same direction as Apple. "She's really tired. Let's let her sleep."

Apple's all-seeing eye, Bicycle thought. Right now, she appreciated it. She said, "Good night, everyone."

She heard what sounded like a fourfold echo:

"Good night."

"Good night."

"Good night."

"Good night."

Bicycle woke the next morning to a gray, rain-drenched light and got a view of the bottom of Daff's bed. She hadn't noticed last night that her family had tucked a little notecard into the wooden slats with a drawing of seven smiley faces and hearts and the words *Welcome Home.*

She thought she might wake up confused by her new surroundings, but she was instantly aware she was an official daughter and sister. She listened to the sounds of raindrops pattering outside and girls breathing softly from the other beds. It seemed she was the first one awake.

At the monastery, she was used to having her own room, tiny as it was. She'd start each day alone, and it was rare to share any conversation with anyone before joining Sister

Wanda and the monks for a mostly silent breakfast. It felt unsettling that someone else might wake up and start talking to her at any moment.

She studied the notecard with the smiley faces. Her parents and sisters had signed their names, and she slipped into her anagram-searching habit. The names Mom and Dad were palindromes, which were neat, but combining them offered nothing more than MOD, MAD, and DAM. She then rearranged the letters in Apple, Banana, Cookie, and Daff, and found CAKE and BAKEOFF, then PEDAL and FLIP. She hummed in satisfaction when she found the fancy word PANACEA, which meant something that cured all problems. She decided to take that as a sign of good things to come.

She hoisted herself to her feet and was surprised to see her mother curled underneath a fleecy bathrobe on the floor. It looked like she'd gone to sleep on the rug next to Bicycle's bed and was still snoozing away.

Bicycle carefully stepped over her and tried unsuccessfully to locate the opening to the room-dividing curtain. She ended up crawling underneath. Seeing the Wheels of Fortune parked amid the clutter made her smile. If she was going to be swept away by life's currents on an unexpected journey, it was good to have a friend along for the ride. They exchanged quiet good mornings, and she crept out the door to the restroom down the hall.

She was splashing some water on her face and rubbing the crusties out of her eyes when the door to the restroom was flung wide. Her mother's whole body looked frantic: wild hair, wild eyes, glasses askew, bathrobe sleeves half off her shoulders.

"There you are!" she gasped. She crushed Bicycle in the kind of hug a drowning person might give a raft. "I woke up and you were gone."

"I needed to use the bathroom," Bicycle mumbled into her mom's arm. Her wet face left a spot on the fleecy bathrobe.

"Oh, yes, of course," Mom said, letting go. She pushed her hair off her forehead. "Whoo! Silly of me, I know." She took a big breath as the door opened again.

Bicycle saw her sisters' faces peeking in.

Mom told them, "I found her! Sorry to get everyone in a tizzy."

Banana said, " 'You' plus 'waking up too early' equals a guaranteed tizzy." She told Bicycle, "Mom and Dad usually sleep double-deep. They told us they're still trying to catch up on lost rest from when we were babies. They say it'll probably take decades."

Mom laughed a strained laugh. "It's true that I'm not at my best first thing in the morning." She patted Bicycle's arm. "I'm sorry, I won't panic every time you use the bathroom. Come on now, who's up for breakfast?"

The morning was filled with explanations and demonstrations about how the girls' homeschool curriculum worked, and Bicycle was glad another thing about her life wasn't changing too much. Teaching time was usually in the mornings so that their parents could work on their freelance textbook editing and crossword puzzle jobs in the afternoons, but sometimes things had to shift around because of chores they needed to do for the commune. For the homeschooling, Mom and Dad traded off on who taught what—Mom handled history, English, and science, while Dad took math, music, and art. They were both good teachers, patient and engaging.

Bicycle tried again to practice her heart-open listening, and made a point to ask Banana what she'd like to be called today. Banana replied, "I might just stick with Banana—so far, inspiration hasn't struck me."

Bicycle asked a few other questions, but didn't feel like she was learning much about her family, even when they weren't in the midst of lessons. The way they talked—interrupting and finishing one another's sentences, going off on new topics and then coming back to the original topic later without warning—made it challenging to take things in.

Before they went to the cafeteria for lunch, Bicycle paused a moment to ask the Fortune for advice on how a person was supposed to get to know their own family.

No data on that particular query, the bike responded.

Here is a list of ice-breaker questions that are frequently used at parties for strangers to get to know one another.

Bicycle memorized the first two. Once everyone had sat down with their food—grilled cheese, salad, and a tomato-and-coconut-milk soup, she dived right in and asked them, "If you woke up tomorrow as an animal, what animal would you choose to be and why?"

"A chameleon," said Dad. "Can you imagine being able to change color?"

"A wolf, so I could howl under the full moon," said Banana. "No, a tiger, so every other animal could be my dinner. No, a polar bear. No, a kiwi. No, a manatee. Come back to me."

"A lioness," said Mom. "I'd sleep in the sun surrounded by my pride."

"A snowy owl, so I could see everything with my enormous eyes," said Daff.

"Did you know some owls' eyes are so big, they take up more space than their brains?" said Apple. "I'd want to be a border collie; they're the smartest type of dog."

"A dolphin because they know how to have fun, but I'd want all of you to be dolphins to have fun with me," said Cookie.

"I've got it!" said Banana. "An otter. No, an octopus. Wait! A bobcat, since they're both tough and cute."

Bicycle wasn't sure what she'd learned with that question,

but it led her to another one. "What do you like to do for fun?" she asked.

The answers ranged from playing board games to making up songs on the piano to reading books out loud to eating to watching animated movies as a family and repeating the lines along with the characters. The family also sometimes played bingo with the commune on Friday nights. That reminded Dad that he'd volunteered to look at the turning mechanism on the bingo-ball turner, and he excused himself from the table.

Bicycle thought about their list of fun activities and noticed that all of them were indoor group activities. She asked, "What about outside?"

Mom and the girls looked at one another.

"We've taken a few homeschooling breaks to get morning snacks at that store in town," Cookie offered. "How about you, what are your favorite fun things?"

"I like to read, and find anagrams, and ride my bike, obviously," said Bicycle. "In fact, I was hoping to go for a ride this afternoon to see the neighborhood, if the rain lets up."

"A ride?" asked Mom, her eyebrows drawing together. "No, honey, the roads around here aren't safe for cycling. Especially not for a young person."

"I was on them a couple of days ago, they seem fine," Bicycle said. "I have lots of experience, I ride defensively, and I always follow correct road rules."

"No." Her mother shook her head. "I'm sorry. I'm not comfortable with that. What if something happened to you?"

Bicycle was about to press her case further when she realized Mom was starting to tear up. Bicycle certainly hadn't meant to hurt her mother's feelings. This wasn't like arguing with Sister Wanda, who might end a discussion by pulling out a book so she could stab authoritatively at facts. Her mother seemed to be taking this very personally.

Apple caught Bicycle's eye with an intense glance that was undoubtedly full of all kinds of identical-sister information. Bicycle tried to beam back the fact she was getting none of it.

Apple finished the conversation for her. "That's okay, Mom, she understands."

Bicycle wished she did. Was she not going to be allowed to ride anywhere?

Ever again?

THE SEVENTH WHEEL

After Dad finished fixing the bingo-ball turner, the family left the cafeteria and returned to their room. Bicycle's sisters decided to divvy up their clothes until Bicycle's stuff came in the mail from the monastery, so they started organizing.

Keeping her voice soft, Bicycle asked Apple, "What did I say that upset Mom?" She didn't want to make the same mistake again.

Apple whispered back, "It's better not to ask to do stuff away from the commune." She handed Bicycle a pair of pants to stick in a drawer.

Cookie quietly added, "I hate seeing Mom and Dad's faces when they tell us no. It's like they're tearing off a big Band-Aid that's gotten stuck to their hearts."

"We tried to convince Mom to let us try public school a few years ago, but she freaked out," Banana said, giving Bicycle a couple of T-shirts.

"But there's lots of fun stuff to do here at Twintopia," said Cookie, pressing a stack of socks into Bicycle's free hand. "We don't need to go anywhere."

Bicycle said, "But not letting me ride my bike . . . that's like asking me not to breathe."

Daff gave her some more shirts.

"There's got to be some way to convince Mom I'll be okay doing it." She didn't think this was being selfish. This was simply being herself.

The four sisters gave her the same slow head shake.

Apple said again, "It's better not to ask."

"C'mon," their Dad called from the other room. "We need to get over to the Lakshmis' place for quad duty in five minutes! Every second we're late deprives Mr. and Mrs. Lakshmi of more sleep!"

Bicycle joined the girls in their rush out the door. Banana explained on the way that "quad duty" meant taking care of infant quadruplet boys. "They're sooo cute, but at least one of them is awake at any given moment. Their parents only sleep when someone comes to give them a break, and it's our turn to help. Not to brag, but we're completely amazing babysitters."

Dad knocked gently on a door decorated with two big bats and four little ones, pushing it open without waiting for a response. Bicycle followed him inside and said, "Holy spokes." Two adults and four bouncy chairs sat on the floor in the middle of a jumble of discarded towels, cartons of formula, towers of diaper boxes, and baby clothes in various states of freshness. The woman had on an inside-out striped pajama top and polka-dot pajama bottoms. The man looked like he'd wrapped a bedsheet around himself as a toga and knotted a couple of burp cloths across the middle as a belt. They were each rocking two bouncy chairs apiece. Both had circles under their eyes so dark they looked like zombies. If Bicycle hadn't known better, she would have guessed they'd dressed up early for Halloween.

"We've got this, Kulsoom and Rahi," Dad said, kneeling down and scooping a fussing baby from one bouncy chair. "You go lie down." Bicycle watched her mom and sisters efficiently gather up the other noisy babies and fill bags with baby paraphernalia. She stayed back, not wanting to do something wrong. She'd never been around a baby before.

"Thank you so much," mumbled the mother. She sank sideways until she was lying flat, resting her head on a Winnie-the-Pooh blanket. She began snoring immediately.

The father started digging in a pile of stuff. "What am I looking for?" he asked hopelessly.

Mom handed him a bottle of water, and Cookie pulled a package of peanut butter crackers from a pocket.

He hugged both to his chest and said, "Bless you."

The Kosroys took the babies down to the communal playroom. Parents and kids were singing songs, patty-caking, and playing dress-up. Bicycle watched how her family rocked and tickled and danced with the quadruplet boys. They traded them back and forth like a well-oiled machine.

Apple asked her, "Want to hold Naveen?" The tiny boy was making warthog-like sounds.

"No," Bicycle said, folding her arms to ward off any attempt to hand her a baby. "I'm afraid I'd break him." Which she was. But she would have said no even if she'd been professionally trained in how to hold infants. She needed to keep a little space to herself. There was only so much closeness and togetherness a person could take. She watched Apple hold up Naveen to the baby in Mom's arms, and the two of them started to sway and bounce in unison. If only Bicycle knew where she fit in to this dance.

Sister Wanda called later that afternoon. "I wanted to see how you are settling in," she said.

"Fine," Bicycle answered. She sat with the family's phone on one of the couches. It was an old-fashioned phone that plugged into the wall with a curlicue cord connecting the handset to the base; her parents said it had come with the classroom. She was hyper-aware that every word she said was easily heard by the six people in the room with her. She didn't want them to listen to her complain about her mother's dismissal of cycling as dangerous, or hear her describe her astonishment at the sounds and substances that came out of quadruplet boys. "It's raining."

"It's raining here, too. Is everyone being kind to you?"

"Yes."

"And I know you're doing your best to be kind to everyone as well."

"Yes."

The rest of the conversation continued the same stilted way. When she and Sister Wanda talked in person, it had always been so easy for Bicycle to say what was on her mind. Or to not say anything at all. Bicycle wished there was a better way to communicate with Sister Wanda while she was here.

That night, when everyone was getting changed for bed, Bicycle decided to wheel the Fortune out into the hall to get a little privacy to chat. Did you ask your family any ice-breaker questions? If so, do you feel any ice has broken?

"I found out which animals they would like to be," Bicycle said.

You have never asked me that question.

"Well, what animal would you like to be?"

Being an animal would not be better than being a bike. Wheels are better than paws, claws, or flippers. However, having a pet could be enjoyable. I would choose a monkey.

"As long as you don't choose a howler monkey. Anyway,

that question broke the ice to find out what they like to do for fun. And that led to me finding out that Mom doesn't want me cycling on the roads. She says the roads here are dangerous."

We can return to the bike trail we took to get here. That is not a road. It continues for another 130 miles to Maryland.

"That's true," Bicycle said. "Although we have to ride on the road to get to that trail."

Perhaps I can use satellite imagery to find a way to travel off-road. Also, riding on the sidewalk is not prohibited in West Virginia. I will check for sidewalk options.

Bicycle was glad the Fortune was willing to get creative. She'd have to think of a way to bring these ideas up to Mom and Dad.

She could hear raised voices inside the apartment: "*What do you mean, you don't know where she is?*"

"*We're sure she's fine, Mom, nothing's wrong.*"

The door flew open and Dad appeared. He sucked in his breath. "Thank goodness, here you are!" Then he called over his shoulder, "Found her!" He turned back to Bicycle and grimaced. "It'd be best if you tell me or your mother when you leave the apartment."

"Sure, no problem," said Bicycle. However, it did turn out to be a problem. For the next several days, Bicycle kept bringing her parents to the edge of panic.

She didn't mean to, of course. She'd feel the urge to have a little alone time and instinctually obey it. She didn't think it would matter if she wandered down a different hallway to seek out some silence when walking back from lunch—until her family came sprinting toward her. She couldn't get used to telling someone when she went to use the bathroom, only remembering she hadn't when Mom banged the restroom door open, shouting her name. Her old life at the monastery had not trained her for this. Other than showing up for homeschooling and helping with chores, the rest of her time had been her own.

Bicycle came right out at one point and told her mom, "Sister Wanda let me ride my bike pretty much anywhere as long as I was home in time for dinner. I'm more used to that kind of freedom."

Mom shook her head and looked to the heavens. She murmured, "Sister Wanda must have nerves of steel." She told Bicycle, "This family runs on togetherness. That's best for us. I already lost you once and I can't . . . I can't . . ." Mom trailed off and bit her bottom lip, eyes filled with pain. "I just can't."

Bicycle knew she was seeing the Band-Aid-peeling face Cookie had mentioned. It hurt to look at; Bicycle scrambled for something to say to make it stop. She borrowed some words Apple had used to reassure their mother a few days before: "It's okay, Mom. I understand." She thought, *I understand that we can't talk about this. I'd better talk to Sister Wanda instead.*

However, Bicycle's short, stilted conversations with Sister Wanda didn't give her the guidance she needed. The nun kept reiterating that Bicycle needed to keep listening to and learning about her family. Bicycle felt like she'd heard at least one thing loud and clear: they needed her to stay close.

She also thought she might be developing a rudimentary version of the mind-reading Quint Sense, but it wasn't a good feeling. Bicycle could tell that her sisters had to scramble to calm Mom and Dad after her inadvertent disappearances. The girls never complained, but rather behaved like they had to clean up a mess Bicycle kept making. It felt like there had been a balance between the six family members before she'd shown up, like a cart with three wheels on each side. She was the odd seventh wheel, throwing it out of whack.

When apartment-cleaning time came around, she looked for a way to show she was a team player. She said, "I'll do whatever everyone's least favorite chore is."

Daff handed her the dusting cloth with a fervent thank-you. Bicycle wiped down the shelves and tables and moved on to clean the Fortune's computer screen.

Did you ask your mom when we can go for a ride? the Fortune blinked.

"It's been raining every day," Bicycle whispered, knowing this was a feeble excuse.

Rain never stopped us before.

"We'll go soon," she said, turning away, not ready to talk about it. She shouldn't be dusting her bike—bikes shouldn't hold still long enough to collect dust. But how could she keep bringing up the idea of riding her bike somewhere alone? That was the opposite of staying close the way everyone wanted her to. Following her urge toward adventure would be selfish. She gave herself a pep talk. *I figured out how to make friends this summer, which wasn't easy. I can figure out a way to fit in with my family.*

She dusted the piano, creating a peculiar tune that sounded like a cat prancing up the keyboard. She dusted a framed picture of Mom and Dad each holding a pair of hiking boots in the air. "What's this photo of?" she asked Apple, who was sweeping rubbish into a dustpan held by Banana.

Apple glanced at it. "Oh, that's from when Mom and Dad met on a walk in the woods."

Dad must have overheard, because he came toward them from the sink with a dripping sponge. "That wasn't just any walk in the woods. I was hiking the two-thousand-mile-long Appalachian Trail, and I was ready to throw in the towel after only a couple of days. Then I met this woman, telling these wild stories around the campfire about how she'd lost all her food in a mudslide, covered her feet in duct tape to stop her blisters from growing more blisters, then outwitted a bear who tried to eat her glasses. And she was grinning when she told them. She said she couldn't wait to see what adventures lay around the next bend in the trail."

Banana shook her head. "What happened to you? You are so not those people anymore." Apple thumped Banana's ankle with the broom.

Dad said, "When you have children, your priorities change. Instead of jumping headfirst into each day, you have to think things through on how you'll keep everyone fed, sheltered, and safe."

"Alex! You are dripping sponge water everywhere," Mom said from the kitchenette area. "Get back over here."

"Coming, dear," Dad replied, then told the girls, "Your mother is still an unstoppable force, don't you forget it."

Bicycle moved on from the hiking photo to dust the framed family portrait of Mom and Dad with their five identical babies arranged on their laps. Mom and Dad were laughing. They looked whole and content, like there was a place for each of them and each of them was in their place. She polished the faces and tried to guess which was hers.

She decided the first Rule for Family Belonging was Find a Place to Fit In. And the second, nearly-as-important one was Ask Before You Use the Bathroom.

*　　*　　*

A big box arrived in the mail from Sister Wanda on Saturday. Surrounded by her curious sisters, Bicycle cut the packing tape and unfolded the top flaps to find her clothes, her postcard collection, her books, her cycling magazines, and her favorite pillow tucked together with military-neat precision. It looked like Sister Wanda had ironed everything that could be ironed, including Bicycle's socks.

Bicycle pulled out her bike repair manual, revealing that Brother Otto had included a container of his famous zucchini muffins, plus what looked like a long, chatty note about the goings-on at the monastery. She saw that the Top Monk had cut out a newspaper article for her about electric bikes and written the word *Sandwich* in the margin, underlined twice. The whole thing made Bicycle feel homesick and comforted at the same time.

Cookie sniffed and peered into the box. "What kind of muffins are those? I can smell nutmeg from here."

"Does that shirt have a bike embroidered on it?" asked Daff.

"You have a copy of *The Phantom Tollbooth*!" Banana said, reaching into the box.

Apple pushed Banana's hand out of the box and said to Bicycle, "Do you want help unpacking, or would you rather go through your things on your own?"

Bicycle hugged her repair manual to her chest and

thought to herself, *Fit in. Be sisterly. Share.* She said, "You can help if you want."

As her sisters pulled out her belongings, asking questions and offering commentary, Bicycle did her best to ignore the part of her that wanted to climb inside the box and close the lid for some peace and quiet.

SLOW DOWN!

The Monday before Halloween, a school bell's *BRIIIIII-ING!* reverberated with the first light of dawn. Bicycle sat up and banged her head on the bottom of Daff's bunk.

"Noooo, not the school bell again," Daff moaned. "Why can't they get that fixed?" The family had mentioned that the building's bell system was supposed to have been disconnected when the commune moved in, but for some reason it occasionally still went off.

Bicycle knew that ring. It was coming not from the school system, but from the Fortune. "No, it's my bike. I'll take care of it." For the first time in a week, the light coming through the windows wasn't dimmed by a sheet of rain. This helped her avoid tripping over her mother, curled up on the braided rug again. Mom was somehow sleeping through the racket.

Bicycle made it over to the raucously ringing Fortune and

pressed a bunch of buttons even though she didn't think it'd help. "Shush, please shush, I'm here. What's wrong?"

The magnet pull is back, though it's fainter than before.

"I don't understand." A shaft of sunlight chose that moment to shine through the room's big windows, making Bicycle squint and shield her eyes "We didn't find anything at the recycling place."

The Fortune's school-bell alarm switched to "Folsom Prison Blues." Johnny Cash sang about hearing the train a-comin', rollin' round the bend, but how he hadn't seen the sunshine since he didn't know when. The music got quieter and quieter through the chorus until the bike went silent. The pull is gone, the Fortune blinked.

"What do you think that meant?" Bicycle asked, taking her hands from her eyes as a cloud swaddled the sunlight. "Are there more bikes that need rescuing somewhere?"

Insufficient data.

"What's up?" four voices chorused behind Bicycle.

She turned. Her sisters had followed her out of bed.

Cookie, fiddling with one of the extra pockets she'd stitched to her pajama top, said, "Is your bike feeling okay?"

"I think so. But it might be getting a message that some other bikes are not. Can we ask Mom and Dad to take us to the scrapyard in West Harpers Ferry right now?" The scrapyard owner had told Sister Wanda there weren't any bikes left to buy, but he might have made a mistake. It seemed like a logical place to check.

Banana shook her head. "Don't you remember how Mom acts when she wakes up too early? Dad's about the same."

I do not know for sure if this was an attempt at communication or some sort of anomaly, the Fortune blinked.

"The Fortune and I can just go before Mom and Dad wake up," Bicycle said. "I remember the way."

"Whoa," said Apple. "First, Mom and Dad would explode from worry if you left here without them."

"Second, after they exploded, Mom would never forgive us if we let you leave here without them," said Banana.

"Maybe we can help you with whatever's going on," said Cookie.

"Can you tell us what *is* going on? Why do you need to go to a scrapyard?" said Daff.

Bicycle explained as much as she thought she understood about her bike being pulled to the scrapyard by messages from bikes in danger of being destroyed.

Banana squinted and said, "I've never owned a bike, but I didn't think they could communicate with each other."

Bicycle said, "The Fortune is unique. It was invented by someone who was trying to create the perfect traveling machine. Sometimes I think there's nothing it can't do, except tell funny knock-knock jokes."

Apple said, "So you haven't gotten a message for over a week, and then it happened again. Why do you think it's coming from the same place? Was it the same music you heard before?"

Bicycle scratched her head. "It was the last song we heard. This time it was shorter, though, and it faded away. Can you play it again, Fortune?"

The bike did so.

Daff asked, "Maybe this message came from Folsom Prison—is that around here?"

It is in northern California.

Bicycle tilted the computer screen so her sisters could see it.

"That's heaps of miles away," said Cookie.

It is 2,814.1257 miles away. We could be there in 235 hours. Everywhere within the continents of North and South America is within biking distance if we have enough time.

"I don't think we should go to California right off the bat," Bicycle said, but something inside her felt a tug. She'd felt pretty adventured-out before coming to Harpers Ferry, but things were different now that even the suggestion of adventure seemed forbidden. Spending 235 hours in the saddle sounded more appealing than spending zero.

Dad parted the curtain and came out yawning. "Good morning, girls." He looked around. "Where is your mother?"

"Our floor," Daff told him.

Their father nodded and shuffled over to start up the coffee maker. "This'll wake her up."

Bicycle decided it couldn't hurt to ask for his help. "Dad, can we go to the scrapyard in West Harpers Ferry today?"

"What for?" He yawned again.

"I . . . heard they have some bikes for sale."

"But you have a bike, and your sisters don't ride." The coffee maker had most of his attention.

Bicycle thought fast. "That's why we need them, so I can teach my sisters to ride. It's good exercise. And a girl needs a bicycle like a fish needs water." Sister Wanda had said that to her once.

Dad grunted in amusement. "The commune property room most likely has a couple for you to share."

Bicycle said, "I think the ones at the scrapyard are really high-quality, though. Could we at least go look?"

Dad watched the stream of coffee dripping down into his mug. "High-quality means out of our price range. Plus, it isn't our turn to use the commune's car. Tell you what: I'll check the property room today and see how many bikes I can dig up." He went back to staring at his dripping coffee.

Bicycle tried but couldn't think of a convincing argument against this. "Okay," she said reluctantly. She crossed her fingers and toes that whoever or whatever had communicated with the Fortune this morning could hang in there until she knew what to do and how to do it.

She tried to look on the bright side: If there were bikes in the community property room, she could teach her sisters how to ride this afternoon. This could be her chance to follow the first Rule of Family Belonging and fit in with her family as the cycling expert.

When Dad came back from the property room that afternoon with four helmets but only one bike, Bicycle's cycling expertise didn't seem like it was going to matter.

Mom looked up from graphing her latest crossword puzzle for the *New York Times*. "What are you doing with that?"

Bicycle was thinking the same thing. The bike Dad wheeled in was the wrong size, probably meant for your average eight-year-old. It had a bell and a cute wicker handlebar basket adorned with bright plastic flowers.

Dad said, "There's so much stuff in that property room, it's the only one I could find. I thought maybe this would be okay for learning on."

"Learning what?" Mom asked.

"How to ride," said Apple, but without enthusiasm.

Bicycle did a double-take: How could anyone look at bike riding without enthusiasm? She then realized Banana and Daff also had resigned expressions on their faces.

Only Cookie's eyes were on the bike. "Is that a bell?" She took the handlebars from Dad. "Can I try it?" She threw her leg over the seat and sat down, her knees bent and feet flat on the floor. She *ding-a-ling*ed the tiny silver bell. "It's perfect."

Bicycle held her tongue. It was far from perfect, but she understood Cookie's smile. Getting on a bike was a magical feeling.

"What on earth made you decide to bring this in here today?" said Mom.

"The girls were talking about bikes this morning, and I told them I'd see what I could find," Dad said. "I didn't realize until Yoof—sorry, Bicycle—came home that we'd never gotten around to teaching the girls to ride. I learned when I was seven, and it was such a great feeling when I raced my friends around the block."

Mom made an exasperated noise. "There's no block for the girls to race around, Alex. I bet you fell down more than once when you were learning. What about scrapes and bruises and, heaven forbid, the possibility of broken bones? And I know the neighborhood where you grew up didn't have the traffic we have today, or distracted drivers on cell phones."

"Guess I didn't think it through," Dad said. "We could use the soccer field—"

Mom interrupted him. "With that high grass, perfect for hiding ticks and snakes? What if someone hits a gopher hole and falls down and gets bitten by an angry gopher swarm? No, I'm not comfortable with it. Please take it back."

Cookie's face fell. "Oh. Are you sure?"

"You know I'm only saying this for your own good. Nothing matters more than my girls' safety," Mom told her. "Going for walks is just as good as biking, and we don't have to leave the commune to do it."

We don't have to leave the commune to do it—Mom's words gave Bicycle an idea. "There is a block for us to ride around," Bicycle said to her mother.

Everyone turned to look at her.

"I can teach them in the hallway. We can follow the loop from the cafeteria. We won't race, we'll go slowly, and do it in the afternoon when the hallways are less crowded." She tried to address the other concerns Mom had raised. "There won't be any ticks, snakes, or gopher holes. We'll wear helmets, and we can even put on other protective gear like shin guards or elbow pads if you have them." She looked at the little bike and then at the Fortune. "I can teach them on my bike instead of this mini one."

"Oh, let's give the little bike a chance!" Cookie said, *ding-a-ling*ing the bell again. "You can just tell it wants a chance. Plus, we're closer to the ground on this one, so we won't fall far if we do fall. Not that we'll fall."

Dad looked willing to give it a shot. Mom looked flummoxed. Bicycle got the sense her daughters didn't often push back when she told them not to do something. But this was something worth pushing about.

"Do you girls want to do this?" Mom asked the sisters.

"Yes, please," Cookie said. "If it's okay with you."

Apple gave Bicycle her penetrating gaze, and seemed to come to some conclusion. She echoed Cookie: "If it's okay with you." She prodded Daff with her elbow.

"You can watch us the whole time," Daff said.

Daff elbow-prodded Banana, who added, "What they said. As long as you agree to call me Brouhaha today."

Mom fluttered her hands. "Well." She took a deep breath and closed her crossword puzzle notebook. "I guess Dad and I can take the afternoon off from work so you can try this. We need to go back to the property room to look for some elbow pads and shin guards."

Bicycle smiled. There was hope.

Cookie went first. Bicycle demonstrated how the pedals and brakes worked, and then stood back to let her get a feel for balancing on two wheels.

Mom stepped in and grabbed the back of the bike seat. "I'll hold on to you and run alongside, how about that, sweetie?"

Cookie shrugged agreeably. However, it quickly became clear that Mom's hunched-over running was too awkward. Bicycle suggested that Mom let go for a minute so Cookie could try "scooting"—pushing the bike along with her feet—to get up enough speed to use the pedals.

Cookie scooted a few feet down the hallway, shouting, "Whee! I just rode across Montana!"

Mom chased her, yelling, "Slow down, for heaven's sake!"

Cookie obediently put on the brakes and the two of them nearly had a collision. Bicycle explained to everyone that in order to learn to ride, you couldn't go too slowly, or you'd never get enough momentum to stay upright.

"I can only bear my girls going fast if I can be right next to them to catch them," Mom protested. "It's a mother's instinct."

"It's a father's instinct, too," said Dad. "I understand. Come on, we can do this together."

She and Dad tried running on either side of Cookie, but Mom couldn't seem to stop yelling, "Slow down!" then yelling, "I'm sorry!" then yelling, "But slow down!"

Cookie was doing her best to accommodate their mother, and Bicycle could see this was a losing proposition.

Cookie relinquished the bike to Brouhaha-Banana. Mom and Dad started fussing over Brouhaha-Banana's shin guards, which she'd put on backward. A few kids emerged from their apartments across the hall to see what the hubbub was all about. One commented, "Bicycling lessons, cool!"

Cookie came over to the other sisters and said quietly, "I thought this would be more fun."

"Once you get the hang of it, it's the most fun," Bicycle said.

Apple joined the conversation. "Mom even yells 'Be careful' at our old home movies, like she can stop us from getting too close to a squirrel eight years ago. We knew this would be tough, but I could tell how much it means to you, so we're going to give it our best try."

"Thanks." Bicycle appreciated knowing her sisters would try to fit in with her at the same time she was trying to fit in with them. She crossed her fingers for Brouhaha-Banana's ride.

Unfortunately, things weren't any easier for the second cycling sister. The girls watched Dad trip over his shoelace and fall to his knees. Then their mother's glasses slid off her nose as she galloped along. She flailed her hands to catch them before they hit the ground and then bumped Brouhaha-Banana's handlebar with her hip, sending the girl careening into the wall.

"My baby!" Mom cried.

"I'm okay!" Brouhaha-Banana called back.

Daff was making a video of the historic moment, but her face said she wasn't sure any of them would want to remember it. "If only there were a way for Mom and Dad to be part of this without . . . being a part of this," she murmured to Bicycle.

Apple went next but quit pretty quickly.

"Oh, man, it looks like I'm up." Daff squared her shoulders like she was going into battle and handed Bicycle her camera. "Can you film this? I can't do both."

Bicycle did her best to focus the shot and thought of a friend she'd made on her cross-country trip: Zbig, the best bike racer in the world. He'd recently opened a bike-racing school, and he'd probably be covering his eyes and exclaiming distressed things in Polish in front of this scene.

After each of the four girls had had a turn, Dad said, "That wasn't like I remember it."

"That wasn't how it was supposed to be," Bicycle told him. "Let me show you." She threw her leg over the Fortune and pumped across Missouri, Nebraska, and Nevada.

"Wait!" Mom yelled. "There's no way I can keep up with you."

Bicycle reluctantly stopped and turned around, ready to say *You don't need to!* But she bit back the words. Disappointment was radiating off her mom in waves.

Daff must have sensed Bicycle's mood because she waved her camera and said, "Hold on. I saw this technique in a movie filmed by rock climbers once. Cookie—got any duct tape?"

Cookie pulled a small roll out of a pocket.

Daff clicked some settings on the camera, then duct-taped it to the front of Bicycle's helmet. "All set to livestream to our computer. The duct tape is covering the microphone, but picking up sound shouldn't be important. Bicycle can ride and we can watch the whole thing inside without having to keep up. If this works, we can take turns using it."

Apple patted Daff's shoulder. "Slick idea, sis."

It took more convincing, but eventually Mom and Dad agreed to try the suggestion and let Bicycle ride the whole fifty-state loop on camera. Their willingness may have had something to do with the fact that they were both sweating heavily.

The kids who'd been watching in the hallway asked, "Is anyone going to fall down anymore?"

"Not anymore," Bicycle told them.

"Oh. The falling down was the best part," one said, and they left.

Once her sisters and parents were set up in front of the computer, Bicycle rolled past Nevada and across New Hampshire, relishing how, even indoors, cyclists make their own breeze.

The Fortune blinked up at her as they blew across New Jersey. Knock knock.

"Who's there?"

A bike with a question.

"A bike with a question who?"

When can we go to the scrapyard to search for the source of the prison song?

"I don't know. Dad said it's not our turn to use the commune's car. There is another problem, though. If we need to rescue some bikes, we may not be able to afford to buy them."

I have all the money we need.

The Fortune made a humming noise as a slit opened in its left handlebar. A freshly printed dollar bill came out. Bicycle plucked it free and tucked it in her pocket, making sure her helmet cam was pointed away from all of this. She would have been amazed if she hadn't seen the Fortune do this before. "You know using counterfeit money is illegal."

It is identical to U.S. currency in every way. You used it to buy ice cream in Nevada.

This was true. No one had ever needed ice cream more than she had in the Great Basin Desert. "I was desperate. I sent the ice cream parlor real money in the mail as soon as we got home. Fake money is not the answer."

Her time in the saddle was over too soon, even with taking a wrong turn after Wyoming and having to backtrack to find Alabama. She wheeled the Fortune into the apartment with fingers crossed to see if Daff's proposal had worked.

Her parents were impressed. "It's like we were right there with you," Dad said. He'd mostly stopped sweating.

Brouhaha-Banana said, "Mom got to yell 'Be careful' at the screen all she wanted."

"Could we each try using it?" asked Cookie. "Bicycle really seems to be good at cycling, and she can coach us. Then you can see we're safe, but you don't have to be right there. Although you can if you want to be."

Dad thoughtfully poked the pile of math textbook pages

awaiting editing on his desk. "This way, we could watch the girls and get some work done at the same time."

Mom looked at her crossword puzzle notebook and then at the clock. "I think this may be okay," she said. "We should get down to the cafeteria for dinner, but if you girls want to try practicing in the hallway again tomorrow, with your sister coaching you one-on-one, you can." She held up one finger. "*If* you promise to wear all your safety gear, and go slowly, and know I'll be out there like a flash if you need me."

"We promise!" Cookie answered, and high-fived Bicycle.

NOT AN ADVENTURE

Dad grumbled the next morning about the return of more rain. "At this rate, our playing fields are never going to dry out before winter."

Mom handed him the coffee creamer. "Cheer up. The radio said this should be the end of the wet weather. Plus, remember what's for breakfast. And lunch. And dinner."

"We get to have two adventures today," Cookie told Bicycle. "Riding bikes with you and Waffle Day."

Bicycle was intrigued. "What happens on Waffle Day?"

"The cafeteria kitchen is open for twenty-four hours, and the World's Biggest Waffle Iron gets brought out of storage," Apple explained.

Daff continued, "Everyone mixes up as much batter as they can, and then we go and take turns pouring waffles into the iron and cooking them up."

"That sounds nice, but I wouldn't call it an adventure," Bicycle said.

"You don't understand," Banana said. "The World's Biggest Waffle Iron makes thirty waffles at one time. And we can go in and make them anytime. Multiple times. Ten o'clock in the morning? Thirty waffles. Three in the afternoon? Thirty waffles. Ten o'clock at night? Thirty more waffles."

Cookie pulled a little jar filled with multicolored particles out of a pocket. "We get to put *sprinkles* in the batter."

Apple added, "There's jugs of real maple syrup. There are cans of whipped cream."

"This day is definitely a good thing," Bicycle said. "But still not an adventure."

"What makes something an adventure, then?" Banana asked.

Bicycle thought. "It has to have some element of the unknown. At least a little bit of risk and excitement. I'd say you have to travel somewhere different, meet unexpected people, or try a new experience."

Cookie said, "It's unknown if we'll run out of syrup."

Apple said, "My new experience will be making a waffle sandwich with whipped cream in the middle."

Daff said, "It turns the commune into a different place— a waffle-filled place—so it's like we're traveling even though we're not going anywhere."

Bicycle felt her face doing something that felt like frowning and smiling at the same time. *Friling? Smowning?* She liked her sisters' enthusiasm about this special day, but she didn't like that their understanding of adventure was so limited. It wasn't worth arguing about, though. "When do we start the cooking?"

When they reached the kitchen, another family was just beginning to tilt the massive waffle iron on its stand. The circular waffle iron was the size of a kiddie swimming pool, mounted on a stand that raised it off the floor. Under the stand, a waxed picnic tablecloth had been spread out. A father cranked a lever on the side of the stand so the iron moved from flat like a table to vertical like a window. "Ready?" he said to his crew, and they said back, "Ready!" He engaged a different lever and the waffle iron creaked open, dumping a mound of heavenly-smelling golden disks onto the tablecloth. Two older kids each grabbed a corner of the cloth and slid it away from the waffle iron. A third child blocked a younger sibling from climbing into the waffle pile headfirst, saying, "Stop! Wait until we get into the cafeteria!"

After the family dragged away their bounty, the Kosroys set to work, showing the same kind of natural coordination they'd had when taking care of the Lakshmis' quadruplets. Apple measured flour; Banana melted butter; Cookie dosed out sugar, salt, and baking powder; Daff beat eggs and poured milk; Mom set up bowls to mix the dry and wet ingredients together; and Dad spread out their own waxed tablecloth and prepped the waffle iron. Bicycle hung back, feeling like a seventh wheel again, until Dad caught her eye and handed her a bottle. "Vanilla. The recipe says it's optional, but it really isn't. Make sure to get a few good glugs of this in the batter. And I do mean glugs—the pitter-patter of a few drops is not the right amount."

Bicycle thought back to making a vat of vanilla pudding with Sister Wanda at the Mostly Silent Monastery. Bicycle had been in charge of the vanilla and had accidentally added twice as much as the recipe called for. She worried that she'd ruined it, but Sister Wanda told her to save the worrying. "With cooking," she explained, "the proof is in the pudding. It often doesn't matter whether you followed the recipe or not, as long as it tastes good." Bicycle remembered that the pudding had proved super-delicious with way too much vanilla—the Top Monk had even pronounced it "sandwich."

Bicycle poured some hearty gurgling glugs of vanilla into the egg-and-milk mixture. Mom got things mixed, and Cookie poured in sprinkles. Bicycle knew she'd done her part right when the waffles cascaded out of the giant waffle iron onto the tablecloth and the vanilla scent filled the air.

The whole family took in a simultaneous breath and let it out with an "Ah!"

They dragged the tablecloth into the cafeteria. Mom doled out plates and utensils. Waffle devouring commenced. Bicycle watched her parents and sisters fill waffle squares with syrup to form designs, the way she'd always done. She tried a whipped-cream waffle, too, which was new to her, and agreed on its scrumptiousness.

Banana layered slices of banana on top of hers. "Not a word from any of you," she said.

Bicycle decided that she needed to bring the Fortune to the next Waffle Day and describe the experience in detail for its database.

The conversation flowed as freely as the syrup. Bicycle felt like she was part of the rhythm this time, sharing stories of cooking with the monks. She even remembered to tell everyone when she left to use the restroom. She was beaming as she walked down the hallway, thinking, *I am getting the hang of this.*

On the way back to the cafeteria, Bicycle caught sight of blue sky out of a window. She gratefully pushed open a door and stepped out for some sunshine. She stood, listening to nothing but her own breath, soaking up the solitary silence. She didn't notice the minutes passing until she heard panicked shouting from inside: *Where could she be? She wasn't in the bathroom! Yoof! Bicycle! Yoofcycle!*

She groaned softly and went back inside to apologize for ruining Waffle Day. If only Mom and Dad could save the worrying until after they knew something had gone wrong, the way Sister Wanda had told her to put worrying on hold until tasting the pudding. The only way she could think of to keep them at ease was to force herself to remember to stay close at all times. She worried that the third Rule of Family Belonging was starting to look like Be Whoever They Need You to Be, Even If It's Someone You're Not.

When it was time for the afternoon bike training, the girls set Mom and Dad up in front of the computer and took the bikes out into the hallway. Bicycle offered again to let her sisters try riding the Fortune, which was the right-sized frame for them, but they all preferred the little bike. "It looks like it would be easier to control," said Cookie.

"At least let me raise the seat," Bicycle said. "Does anyone have an Allen wrench?"

Cookie pulled a folding multitool out of a pocket and watched over Bicycle's shoulder as she loosened and pulled the seat post out to its maximum height. Bicycle showed her how to re-tighten the seat.

When they stepped back, Banana said, "Me first, okay?" She didn't wait for an answer from anyone before climbing on the bike and fastening the helmet cam on her head.

"We're going to do this right," Bicycle told Banana,

getting on the Fortune. "Mirror exactly what I do, at exactly the same speed."

Banana watched Bicycle like a hawk and was pedaling and balancing upright in no time, able to stop and catch herself whenever she wobbled. "I'm queen of the world!" she yelled at the end of the hallway. "Are there any famous bike racers whose names begin with *B*?"

"There's Beryl Burton. She shattered road riding records in the 1960s," said Bicycle.

Banana crowed, "Call me Beryl today! Can we keep going?"

"Let's do the whole loop," Bicycle said. They went through all the *N* states, the *O* states, the one *P* state, Beryl-Banana mirroring Bicycle and gaining confidence with each rotation of the wheels.

"I'm kind of amazing at this, huh?" Beryl-Banana said. "I mean, I'm identical to you, so it's no surprise."

They made one full loop past the cafeteria and back to the apartment. Cookie waved them down, saying, "Me next."

Beryl-Banana replied, "I forget how to stop!" and kept going. Bicycle followed her to explain the brakes again and Beryl-Banana told her, "I know, I know, I just wasn't ready to stop yet." They started the loop again. "You know where I'd ride this bike if I could?"

This seemed like a perfect ice-breaker question: *Where*

would you ride a bike if you could? Bicycle wished she'd thought of it before. She then realized this was the first conversation she'd had with Beryl-Banana without the rest of their sisters around. She'd been getting to know her sisters in a clump—here was a chance to get to know them one-on-one. "Where would you go?" she asked.

"To a karate class. I think I'd be really, really good at attacking people in a controlled and graceful way. I saw it on television a few times and I'm pretty sure I can do it. Ki-yah!" she yelled and flung one arm through the air, losing control of the bike and careening into the wall. Her front tire bounced off it as she squeezed the brakes hard. She put her feet on the ground and bowed to the wall. "Karate Cyclist respects you as a worthy opponent."

Bicycle said, "Quick, turn and look at me." She gave the helmet cam a thumbs-up, hoping their parents would see this and know they didn't have to come running to save anyone. "Now, don't forget to keep both hands on the handlebars, and look where you want to go," she admonished Beryl-Banana as her sister started pedaling again. "Your bike follows your face."

"This is why I need a karate class. The teachers can show me how to direct my raw power."

"Have you asked Mom and Dad if you can try it?"

Beryl-Banana answered, "It's better not to ask. Besides,

we'd all have to go, and Apple, Cookie, and Daff don't want to do it. That's when it's cruddiest to have Quint Sense—trying to have fun while your sisters are suffering next to you. Wi-yah!" She took a foot off a pedal and did a front kick. "No one sees Karate Cyclist coming."

A Karate Cyclist would be a fearsome foe, blinked the Fortune. She could strike and speed away. Your sister is interesting.

"I'll show you how to be a regular cyclist first," said Bicycle. She felt sad that her sister wouldn't even ask to try something she really wanted to do. *Well,* she reminded herself, *I can't make it easier to ask our parents things, but I can help here and now.* "Try to center yourself and not lean to either side."

She advised Beryl-Banana on technique, and listened to her talk about how when karate practitioners fought, they knew how to refrain from actually injuring each other.

Beryl-Banana said, "I don't want to beat people up, just use cool moves on them."

They came in sight of their sisters.

"Unless I had to defend my family. Then watch out—ki-YAH!" Beryl-Banana tried a jab-and-kick combo that took her into the wall again. This time she ended up on the floor just outside of their apartment.

Bicycle stood over her and gave the camera a double-thumbs-up and a smile. She could feel her sisters taking in a collective breath and waiting to see if Mom and Dad would rush out into the hall to check on their girls. But the door stayed closed.

This was going to work.

HELP US

Cookie walked over and picked up the too-small bike, saying, "My turn now."

"What if I were injured?" Beryl-Banana said, dramatically putting her hand to her heart.

"Quint Sense, remember? I know you're fine. Hand over the helmet cam, Banana."

"Beryl is my new name today," she told Cookie before turning to Bicycle. "Thanks for the lesson, coach. Way better than Mom and Dad running and yelling."

"You bet," Bicycle told her. She was curious how the other training rides would go. "Ready, Cookie?"

Cookie *ding-a-ling*ed the silver bell. "Ready! What do I do first?"

"I'll show you. Mirror exactly what I do, at exactly the same speed." They started slowly down the hallway. "While we're going, think about your answer to this question: If you could ride this bike anywhere, where would you want to go?"

Cookie said dreamily, "That's easy. The farmers' market eating contest! The farmers' market is every Saturday except in winter, and once a month there's an eating contest." Cookie lowered her voice so Bicycle had to strain to hear. "Don't tell anyone this, but any day other than Waffle Day, I want to eat one more of whatever I get. It's not that I'm always hungry— I just love food. I don't want to be greedy, so I usually don't say anything after I finish my bowl of popcorn or my pork chop. It'd be terrific to be given so much food it seems like you can't finish it all." She looked into the distance. "*I* could finish it all."

"Why not see if Mom and Dad will let you enter the contest?"

"I don't want to do it with everyone, and that's the only way we do everything. You know how we have Quint Sense? When one of us picks an activity that bores or annoys the rest of us, the pressure of sensing all that boredom and annoyance squishes the fun out of it."

"Beryl mentioned that, too," Bicycle said.

"I especially don't want Mom and Dad watching me eat. I'd have to use good table manners, instead of letting my mouth and hands fly free." She looked down at the little bike. "Am I doing this right?"

"You are."

Cookie was a more careful rider than Banana, so they took their time. Bicycle figured that beyond cycling, she was also good at listening, so she listened to Cookie talk more about eating. She found out that the only food Cookie wouldn't enter a contest for was eating hot dogs.

"I like hot dogs, but the way competitive eaters snarf them down so fast is they dip the buns in water to squash them. That is plain gross."

The Fortune blinked, I would not like anyone to describe that in detail to me. However, I would like to observe if Cookie can consume the mass quantities she thinks she can. Two of your sisters are interesting.

They were coming around to the end of the loop. One sister ran up to Cookie and held her hand out in a "stop" gesture. "My turn now. I'm totally Daff, and I am next in line."

"No, you aren't, you impostor," said the real Daff, poking the Daff pretender. "You got to do two loops, you do *not* get another turn before me and Apple."

The impostor, Beryl-Banana, shrugged. "Can't blame a girl for trying."

Cookie thanked the too-small bike for the ride before handing it and the helmet cam over to Daff. She then started searching her pockets. "Bike riding makes me hungry," she said, pulling out a waffle in a baggie. "Want a piece?" she asked Bicycle, tearing off a hunk.

"Bike riding makes everyone hungry, especially if you talk about food while you're doing it," Bicycle said, accepting the hunk. She turned her attention to coaching Daff.

Daff wanted Bicycle to recite her advice twice before they started trying to ride. Then as they started to ride, she muttered, "I knew I would learn, but how quickly? I focused on my sister's instructions like a laser." She then repeated Bicycle's advice to herself under her breath. Bicycle waited until she got quiet and then asked the ice-breaker question. It turned out that Daff wished she could go by herself to see the Halloween Horror Movie Festival at the Movie House in Harpers Ferry.

"They're showing classic creepy movies all day and all night, including *Dracula*, a few different versions of *Frankenstein*, and some Alfred Hitchcock. At the film festival, I could study how horror filmmakers build suspense. I'd like to try making my own films, with scripts and plots, instead of just recording Historic Moments with the Kosroy Family. If Mr. and Mrs. Lakshmi don't mind, I'm hoping to use their babies in a movie I'll call *Night of the Quadruplets*. I'm halfway through the script already."

"Why not make *Night of the Quintuplets* starring us?" Bicycle joked.

"Twelve-year-olds aren't as scary as babies," said Daff. "No one knows what a baby might do next, including the baby."

"I bet you don't want to ask Mom and Dad if you can go to the film festival," Bicycle guessed.

"Nooooope," said Daff, drawing out the word. "We'd have to go to it together, which won't work. Even the tamest horror movies give Dad and Apple nightmares. Plus, the one time I convinced the whole family to attend the Classic Westerns Film Festival at a movie theater in New Jersey, my Quint Sense was on fire with how bored and restless our sisters felt. They didn't even like *The Good, the Bad, and the Ugly*. Do you know that one?"

Bicycle did, from watching it with the Mostly Silent Monks, who appreciated how the actor Clint Eastwood could communicate a whole lot by saying very little.

"How could anyone be bored by that?" Daff continued. "No one else in our family appreciates that all well-made movies—westerns, horror movies, it doesn't matter—are art. We mostly watch animated films at home, which are fine, but not enough for me."

Daff went on to explain things that she'd read about in books: camera angles and framing shots, and the importance of soundtrack music. "Music in movies helps the audience to understand what is going on. I wish we could have background music in real life." Daff gushed about the genius of movie-score composer John Williams, who used powerful themes in music to hint about what was coming next and reveal characters' emotions. "He's scored dozens of great movies, including *Star*

Wars, which Mom let me watch once when I was sick with the flu. He also created the super-sinister theme from *Jaws*. I listened to that score online and it gave me goose bumps."

The Fortune played the famous a-great-white-shark-is-swimming-toward-you melody from *Jaws*. Bicycle hadn't seen the movie, but she knew this menacing music. *DA-duh. DA-duh. Dun-duh-dun-duh-dun-duh-dun-duh* . . . A kid was opening his apartment door ahead of them. He startled and said in a shocked voice, "The shark bike is coming to get us!" Then he slammed the door.

The Fortune blinked, Maybe you can ask if I can star in a movie called *Shark Bike*. Perhaps Daff can build suspense about whether I am a bike or a shark. Three of your sisters are interesting.

When they got back to their front door, Apple pushed Beryl-Banana out of the way before she could pretend it was her turn again. Apple switched places with Daff and said, "Before we start, can you tell me the physics behind why bicycles balance when they're in motion but fall down when they stop?" She had a little notebook and a pencil.

Bicycle tossed this question over to the Fortune, whose screen filled with details on gyroscopic theory.

It added, Cycling is a partnership between a rider and a bike. We need each other to move forward.

"Cool beans," said Apple, writing this down. "How can I be a good partner?"

Bicycle gave her the same instructions as her sisters. Apple put the notebook and pencil in the little bike's wicker basket, and they set off. Apple asked a lot of questions about how to properly sit on the seat, grip the handlebars, align her shoulders, and push the pedals. She kept stopping to take notes. Around North Carolina, the Fortune offered to keep track of the conversation for her so she could write it down at the end, which she agreed would work better.

Bicycle was hoping they wouldn't spend their whole time talking only about cycling technique, and was glad when Apple brought up the ice-breaker question on her own. "I know what you're going to ask me—where would I ride this bike if I could go anywhere I wanted?"

"Did Beryl and Cookie tell you I asked them that?"

"They did." A light sparkled in Apple's eyes.

Bicycle wondered if Apple would be the sister to answer with a glamorous, exotic dream destination. Maybe she'd want to bike to another state, like Alaska, or another country, like Canada, or another continent, like Africa.

"I want to walk a dog," Apple said breathlessly. "I don't care what kind of dog. The website for the animal shelter in town says they'll accept junior volunteer dog walkers that are ages twelve and up and over five feet tall to walk dogs weighing less than twenty-five pounds. I'd bike there and tell them: Give me a fluffy dog like a Shetland sheepdog, a short-hair dog like a beagle, or a tiny dog wearing a sweater like a chihuahua. I can walk with anybody."

"Doesn't anyone in the commune have a dog you could walk?"

Apple shook her head. "No one here owns a pet beyond a few goldfish. I think our families have their hands full taking care of their kids. Did you know that dogs with ears that stand up straight are closer genetically to wolves, and dogs with floppier ears have been domesticated longer?" She outlined the history of dogs and humans. "When I have my own house, I'm going to have two dogs, a cat, an indoor bunny, and a flock of chickens. The chickens won't be indoors, though, because of the mess they'd make. Except maybe if one of them wasn't feeling well and needed special care. If you need to keep a chicken indoors, she can wear an invention called a chicken diaper."

I have never learned so much on such a short ride, the Fortune blinked. All of your sisters are interesting. However, I do not share Apple's enthusiasm for dogs. They tend to regard bikes as something to chase. Perhaps she can look into chicken walking instead. It played a chorus of "The Chicken Dance."

"You haven't asked Mom and Dad about doing dog walking because they'll say dogs are too dangerous, right?" said Bicycle.

"Right. Mom has a scar on her chin from an accidental dog bite. She doesn't want us too close to any creature with sharp teeth and a mind of its own," Apple said. "Plus, the entire family would have to do it together, and how would that work? We'd have to take turns walking the dog, or we'd have to each walk a dog from the shelter at once. Mom would never let us be around that many dogs." She sighed. "One of our neighbors told me their twins were dressing up as puppies for trick-or-treating and that they'd let me walk them with those kid harnesses." She shook her head. "It wouldn't be the same."

The Fortune switched to playing "Who Let the Dogs Out?" They crossed Maine, Maryland, Massachusetts, Michigan, Minnesota, and Mississippi, Bicycle thinking to herself that it didn't matter who let the darn dogs out. It mattered who would let her sisters out. Would they have to grow into adults before they could have individual adventures—even very small, very tame adventures? Too bad Bicycle had to focus on how to fit in and be the person her family needed her to be—she could have taught Apple, Beryl-Banana, Cookie, and Daff a lot more than how to balance on two wheels.

When cycling practice was over, the girls went back into the apartment to find their parents math-editing and crossword-puzzling side by side in front of the computer screen. Their mother looked up and did a double take. "I just saw myself on the screen when you walked in. I'm sorry I didn't come out into the hallway to check on you—it turned out to be so interesting to see things from your perspective."

Apple took off the helmet and shut down the camera.

"It didn't make you want to run out and catch us?" Beryl-Banana asked.

"It was a little confusing at a couple of points, but then we'd see Bicycle looking confident, so that helped," Dad said. "My favorite part was when each of you turned the camera toward your sisters. Want to hear something funny? It was hard to tell you apart on video—thank goodness we never had that problem in real life."

"You really never mixed them—us—up?" Bicycle asked. With identical kids, this seemed bound to happen.

Apple explained, "They say our voices are unmistakable. One time for Halloween we dressed up in identical outfits. That threw them at first, but as soon as we said 'Trick or treat,' it was like we'd painted our names on our foreheads."

Bicycle asked, "What about when we were really little?"

Mom said, "Even when you could babble only nonsense sounds, you were unique. Apple would sigh, Banana would grunt, Cookie would peep, Daff would gurgle, and you would moo."

"I would *moo*?" Bicycle said.

"There's no better word for it," Mom said. "We'll dig out some home videos and let you listen."

"It's a shame our voices stopped us from pulling any *Parent Trap*–type capers on anyone," said Daff.

Dad said, "It's been a huge relief. When the doctors tell you you're having identical quintuplets, one of the first things you worry about is mixing them up. Watching you in the silent movie from the helmet cam was definitely strange. So, what's the verdict?" he asked Bicycle. "Are your sighing, grunting, peeping, gurgling sisters going to be good cyclists?"

"They are picking it up fast," Bicycle said. "When we can find them bikes that fit properly, they'll be great."

"I'll check the property room again when I get the chance," promised Dad.

That night as the girls lay in bed, Beryl-Banana said, "We realized none of us asked *you* the question of where you'd ride your bike if you could go anywhere you wanted. So, what's your dream ride?"

Bicycle had many answers to that. "I've pedaled in ten states, so the next forty are on my list, starting with this famous group ride across Iowa. I want to ride from Vancouver down the Pacific Coast to Mexico. I want to ride the route of the Tour de France. I want to ride in Poland, New Zealand, Japan, and Holland. For starters."

The four other girls chorused, "Wow."

Apple added softly, "Those rides sound . . . epic."

Bicycle continued, "I'd also want to go back and visit the places I went this summer to see my friends again."

Daff asked longingly, "What was it like to go adventuring on your own?"

Bicycle told them tales of meeting kind folks, eating excellent food, seeing stunning sights, and sometimes wanting to give up but discovering the path to the next pedal stroke forward. They listened in spellbound silence until sleep claimed them.

Bicycle's dream that night was that she and three of her sisters had turned into animals: Banana was a pig, Cookie was a chick, Daff was a fish, and Bicycle herself was a cow. She was trying to teach them how to ride but could only moo instead of speak. Apple kept looking at them and sighing, "We'll never make it across Iowa now." She was almost glad when a bright and brassy school-bell alarm let out a BRIIIIIING! at dawn the next morning to wake her up.

Daff asked sleepily, "Is that the building or your bike again?"

"It's my bike, sorry." Bicycle stumbled through the curtain to the Fortune's side. She whispered, "Is it another message? Did you find something out?"

The Fortune's speakers stopped ringing and played a strange snippet of music. It sounded like five different words sliced from five different songs to form a phrase. It repeated and Bicycle listened hard.

Help. Us. We. Are. Trapped.

"Holy spokes," Bicycle said. "What does that mean?"

Someone is trapped.

"Who is? Fortune, can you ask them who they are?"

I will try.

The Fortune was quiet as it concentrated. A different snippet of music played.

Wolf. Hid. Us. Will. Melt. Us.

Bicycle jammed her fingernails into her palms. "It sounds like some bikes are going to be melted at Wolff's scrapyard. Can you ask if that's right?"

I am working on it. This is not easy.

Morning. Sunbeam. Hits. Window. Short time. Power. Will. Shut. Off. Soon. Please. Come. The sound became quieter.

"Come where?" Bicycle said.

Help. Us.

The speakers fell silent.

A FORTUNE OF FORTUNES

"That was weird," chorused four voices behind Bicycle. Her sisters had followed her out of bed.

"Did you hear the whole thing?" she asked.

Banana summed things up. "Someone needs help getting out of a trap and there's a wolf involved."

"Wolff is the last name of the scrapyard owner. I was right. The message must be coming from there," Bicycle said.

Apple said, "Can I ask your bike a question?"

Bicycle made a be-my-guest gesture, and Apple approached the Fortune.

"Good morning. Do you get your energy from the sun?" She read the Fortune's reply on its screen.

No. My energy comes from static electricity. Some earlier Wheels of Fortune models were solar-powered, but our inventor realized this limited our capabilities.

Apple asked Bicycle, "Did you notice that message said something about a sunbeam hitting the window for a short time and then power shutting off? It made me think that maybe the message-sender was using solar power to communicate."

Cookie added, "It also said they'd been hidden. They might be somewhere that only gets a little sunshine."

"It mentioned morning sun." Banana snapped her fingers. "That's why you haven't heard anything for a while, because it's been crazy rainy. They didn't have enough solar energy to keep talking to you. See? We've got it figured out."

Incoming data, the Fortune blinked. I have accessed the scrapyard security video link. Images of the scrapyard flitted across its screen: the cranes, the piles of stuff, the trailer. A small shed marked PRIVATE came up on the screen. There, the Fortune blinked. The transmission came from in there.

It zoomed in closer on the image, centering on the shed's one window. Most of the glass was clouded by grime, but one slim section was clear—a section so slim it probably let in no more than a brief shaft of morning sunlight. The Fortune zoomed in another level, and Bicycle choked at what she saw inside.

Four bikes. Inside the shed there was just enough light to see the names emblazoned across their top tubes in gold.

The Wheels of Fortune 713-A. The Wheels of Fortune 713-B. The Wheels of Fortune 713-C. The Wheels of Fortune 713-D.

No wonder these bikes could communicate with hers. They'd been made by the same inventor.

On her cross-country trip, Bicycle had met the inventor of the Wheels of Fortune, a brilliant scientist named Dr. Luck Alvarado, who had been hired by the government to create a perfect traveling machine. She knew he'd made several versions of the bicycles, improving each new one with added abilities. He'd included a lot of features that the government didn't care about, like music databases and the ability to track the rider's good and bad luck, and had refused to add features they did care about, like machine guns. They'd canceled his contract and never picked up most of the bikes.

The Fortune blinked, We are getting them out. Failure is not an option.

Bicycle couldn't begin to guess how these four bikes had ended up here, but she agreed with the Fortune—not saving them was not an option. These were essentially her bike's family, after all. She told her sisters, "Those bikes cannot, cannot, cannot get melted."

Apple said, "Let's call the scrapyard and ask if we can buy them. Maybe they thought no one wanted them."

Bicycle recognized this was a good idea, even though her instincts were telling her to leap onto the Fortune and pedal headlong into a rescue mission. Cookie peeked in at their parents and reported they were still conked out. Daff looked up the number and Bicycle tapped it into the phone, hoping someone would answer at this early hour. Her sisters crouched close around her so they could listen as well.

"Wolff's Scrapyard, Chuck speaking." Bicycle was expecting to hear Mr. Wolff's deep, gravelly voice. Chuck sounded quite different—younger and somehow wispier.

"May I please speak to Mr. Wolff?" she asked.

"My father's not here today. He said he could hear some striped bass begging him to come fishing."

"Oh, okay. I wanted to buy the four bikes you have."

"The bikes are gone, sold or scrapped, sorry. Have a nice day."

"Wait!" Bicycle wished she'd planned what she was going to say before she'd dialed. "I think you might have made a mistake. I know that some were . . . set aside."

Chuck's wispy voice got cagey. "You heard that, huh? From who? I'm telling you, everything was sold."

"But . . . but . . . I really . . ." This was not going well.

Banana grabbed the phone from Bicycle. "Look, sir, I'm a busy woman. Let's get down to business. It doesn't matter how I know you've got some bikes, just that I do, and that I want them. Are we making a deal this morning or what?"

This made Chuck laugh. "I already have a deal, and I doubt you can beat it. You got more than four hundred thousand dollars?"

Apple, Cookie, Daff, and Bicycle gasped.

Banana seemed unfazed and declared, "Four hundred thousand is chump change to me. I spend a half million every month to swap out my gold-plated limousine for a fresh one. But I need to be sure these bikes are worth it. These are the solar-powered kind, right?"

"I don't know, but I could tell right away they weren't ordinary bikes. Can't believe we only paid twenty bucks for the lot. I had their frame metal tested and found a lab that'll pay top dollar for the chromoly titanium they're made out of. I'm going to strip the frames of the extra pieces before I melt them for the lab."

"When are you melting the frames?"

"A week from Friday, when the crucible arrives."

"I'll be down there before then with cash in hand," Banana told him. "Don't sell those bikes to anyone but me."

"And your name?" Chuck asked.

"Belladonna Kosroy. Don't you forget it." Belladonna-Banana slammed down the phone. "And that's how it's done."

"How *what* is done?" Bicycle asked. "Why did you say those things?"

"Pretty good, right?" Belladonna-Banana grinned. "Daff had me practice some lines from her script for *Night of the Quadruplets*, and I was channeling the obnoxious billionaire who gets eaten in the opening scene."

"I don't think that helped," Bicycle said.

"Of course it did. We know that he's not going to melt the bikes for a week and a half," Belladonna-Banana said.

"But we're not going to come up with four hundred thousand dollars by then," Bicycle said. Then she considered that her family might have some secret stash of jewels they could sell in an emergency. "Are we?"

"Apple will figure something out," Belladonna-Banana said breezily. "She's the smart one."

Apple said, "We're equally smart, you dope. And smartness has nothing to do with the ability to pull money out of thin air." She looked sadly at Bicycle. "I don't think there's anything we can do. Let's get dressed."

Bicycle nibbled a fingernail. She knew someone who could pull money out of thin air. Sort of. While her sisters were changing, she wheeled the Fortune over to the corner of the apartment farthest from the bedrooms to talk.

The Fortune had heard everything. It blinked, Dr. Alvarado used nothing but the best materials in us. Those Wheels of Fortune models deserve a better fate. We must free them.

"You're right," Bicycle told it. "We will find a way."

Or we will make one.

The Fortune printed a bill. Bicycle grabbed it fast. She saw the denomination in the corner: $100,000. She had no idea that bills came in such large denominations. The bike printed three more, and she stuck them in her pocket with

138

the single dollar bill from the other day. This time, she didn't scold her bike about creating counterfeit money.

Bicycle fidgeted with her lentils and rice over lunch. She tried saying things in her head, like *Hey, I happened to find four one-hundred-thousand-dollar bills in the hall. Can we use them to buy these awesome bikes?* She couldn't imagine Mom and Dad saying what she wanted them to say next: *What good luck! Of course we'll use the money to buy those awesome bikes!* There was no way any responsible adult would embrace a windfall like this without some serious questions.

As usual, the conversation popped around the table like popcorn cooked in a pot with no lid. Bicycle didn't do a very good job of talking, or of listening, either. There didn't seem to be any way around it—she was going to have to somehow go to the scrapyard by herself and buy the bikes' freedom, even if it meant going against her family's rules. She wished she could talk to Sister Wanda about this. She thought about how she'd snuck off and done things that were against Sister Wanda's rules in the past—for instance, taking off on a cross-country bicycle journey instead of going to camp. Of course, she'd known Sister Wanda wouldn't be thrilled, but she hadn't worried that her actions might hurt the nun or ruin their relationship.

When bike-riding practice time came around, she was still jittery and discombobulated. She kept hearing the words *Help us* echoing in her head.

The Fortune blinked at her, *I want to go right now. Can we go now? Let us go right now. I can use my Pied Piper setting to lead the bikes home: any Wheels of Fortune bike can use a radio signal to guide the others along a road even if they have no riders.*

I can't do this, and I can't not do this, Bicycle thought. "How long would it take us to get there and back?"

An hour at most. We are fast.

An hour wasn't much. Doing one against-the-rules thing didn't mean she was choosing to be a rule breaker forever. In fact, if she didn't try to save the Fortunes, she'd be too miserable to follow the Rules of Family Belonging. She told herself, *I'll do it. But after this, I'll go right back to working hard at being a well-behaved, stay-close daughter.* That way, Mom and Dad could enjoy the pudding of living with her, never needing to know the recipe, which included a dash of adventure and a glug of independence.

Not getting caught was the trick, though. There might be a way, but she couldn't do it alone.

Bicycle and her sisters went out into the hallway. Her sisters did rock-paper-scissors to determine who would cycle first today. Belladonna-Banana cut Apple's paper, covered Cookie's rock, and crushed Daff's scissors.

"What are we learning today, coach?" Belladonna-Banana asked Bicycle, strapping on the helmet cam.

"What do you do when one of you really needs help?" Bicycle asked.

"We help, duh," said Belladonna-Banana.

"We're sisters," said Cookie.

"We've got each other's backs," said Daff.

"What do you need help with?" asked Apple, cutting to the chase.

Bicycle bit the bullet and asked, "Can you cover for me so I can ride to the scrapyard right now and rescue those bikes?"

"Oh, no," said Cookie. "What if Mom comes out here? What are we supposed to say?"

"That I'm in the bathroom?"

"Like that helps," said Daff. "She'd just go look for you in there."

Bicycle said, "Maybe tell her my stomach's upset and I need some alone time. I only need you to do this for a little over an hour." She figured it couldn't take very long to hand over the money. "Please."

Apple shook her head no. Then she paused her shaking and frowned into space. "Wait. Wait one second." She gave Bicycle a hard look. "You're not scared of doing this? You really think you can pull it off? What about the money?"

"I'm not scared. I have to try. I'm going to jump out of my skin knowing those bikes are in danger of being melted when I might be able to stop it." Bicycle hated to lie about the counterfeit money, but she didn't see any way around it. She fudged by saying, "I'll find a way to persuade Chuck."

Apple tapped her lips with one finger. "There's only one way to see if it'll work. Give us a thumbs-up," she said.

"Huh?" said Bicycle.

"Show us exactly how you gave the helmet cam a smiling thumbs-up yesterday to show our parents confidence," said Apple. "We need to duplicate it if we're going to pretend to be you. You heard Mom and Dad say they couldn't tell us apart on video." Apple exchanged an enigmatic glance with Belladonna-Banana, Cookie, and Daff. After a moment, each of them nodded.

Bicycle gave them the most heartfelt thumbs-up ever. "I owe you big-time," she said as they emulated her.

"We're sisters," said Cookie.

"We've got each other's backs," said Daff.

"I'm Bicycle," said Belladonna-Banana in a high-pitched voice that sounded nothing like any of them. "I'm foolhardy but brave, and I love bikes. I will do everything I can to not get my sisters in trouble."

"No, I'm Bicycle first, you can be Bicycle next," said Apple. "Go," she said to Bicycle. "We've got this. Don't be late."

We are fast, the Fortune blinked again.

"We'll fly like the wind," Bicycle promised.

A RESCUE

Bicycle and the Fortune raced away from Twintopia like they were being chased. Luckily, it was downhill most of the way to the scrapyard. (Bicycle tried not to think about what that meant for the way back.) They arrived at the weathered plywood sign on the chain-link fence in twenty-two breathless minutes.

As soon as they were through the gate, the Fortune let out a concert-level wail of R&B music. Passionate vocalists sang about no mountain being high enough, no valley low enough, and no river wide enough to keep them from getting to you.

"Is that a new message from the other Fortunes?" Bicycle asked.

No. It was from me to them. I wanted the bikes to know we are here to perform a rescue.

A young man wearing a cowboy hat and chewing on a

toothpick came out from behind an old, upside-down school bus. He saw Bicycle and looked perplexed. "Were you . . . singing?"

"Yes," Bicycle answered. "That was me. Mountains and valleys, woo-hoo!"

She saw the name embroidered on the young man's blue coveralls—this was Chuck. Where Mr. Wolff had a beard and a ponytail, Chuck was clean-shaven and no hair at all peeked out from under his hat.

"Can I help you?" Chuck asked.

Bicycle pushed the Fortune behind her. She didn't want him looking too closely at it. She said what she'd planned out on the way: "I, er, work for Belladonna Kosroy. You spoke to her earlier about four bikes she'd like to buy from you."

"Oh, yeah." Chuck scratched his chin and shifted his toothpick from one side of his mouth to the other. Bicycle noticed that it wasn't an ordinary toothpick, but an extra-thick one with a word burned into it: TOUGH.

Bicycle tried to think of how an eccentric millionaire's assistant might behave. She straightened her spine and put on an impatient face. "Ms. Kosroy sent me down here with four hundred thousand and one dollars to get those bikes today."

Chuck snorted. "Four hundred thousand and one dollars in cash?"

"Cold, hard cash," said Bicycle, although the bills in her pocket were now hot and wilted with sweat.

Chuck's eyebrows climbed up his forehead. "She sent a kid here with that kind of money? I don't believe it."

Bicycle pulled out a one-hundred-thousand-dollar bill and waved it at him. "Believe it. Ms. Kosroy doesn't mess around."

Chuck's eyebrows climbed even higher, disappearing under his hat brim. He pulled a rag out of his back pocket and wiped his hands with it, then reached for the bill. Bicycle gave it to him, hoping the Fortune knew what it was talking about when it said it was identical to U.S. currency in every way. She'd already made up her mind that she'd anonymously mail Chuck twenty real dollars—the price he'd originally paid for the Fortunes—to make up for passing him the counterfeit dough.

Chuck rubbed it with his thumbs and forefingers and bit down hard on his toothpick. The money must have been close enough to real for him. "I knew those bikes weren't ordinary, I knew it right off the bat. Dad never needs to know about any of this," he said mostly to himself. "Okay, kid. Your boss has got a deal." He held out his hand for the rest of the money. "Have your truck come around to the east entrance and I'll load everything up for you."

"Right, our truck," said Bicycle. She said the first thing that bounced into her mind. "It's not available now because it's . . . picking up a delivery of pigs." She didn't want the Fortune to demonstrate that Pied Piper setting in front of

Chuck. The less he understood about how amazing and unusual these bikes were, the better.

"Your boss deals in pigs and bikes? What kind of business is she in?" He'd fanned out the money to admire it.

Bicycle imagined what Belladonna-Banana might say. "If you don't know what pigs and bikes have in common, I don't have time to explain it to you," she said. This felt a bit rude. Then she remembered that this guy was going to melt her bike's family and decided rudeness might be called for.

Chuck didn't seem insulted. "I can deliver them to you tomorrow in the a.m. to any location within ten miles. Extra charge, though, twenty-five dollars."

"No problem," Bicycle said, giving him Twintopia's address and mentally adding twenty-five more dollars to the amount she'd mail him. She knew she was supposed to feel bad about breaking the law, but couldn't quite manage it. In this case, she felt certain the law would make an exception for the Wheels of Fortune if it knew they existed.

Chuck dug out a stubby pencil and receipt booklet. He signed and dated a receipt; had Bicycle sign it, too; and pulled off one copy for her to keep. "See you tomorrow." He turned to leave.

Bicycle realized she'd been so focused on making the deal that she hadn't even seen the bikes yet. "Wait—I forgot that Ms. Kosroy told me I should inspect the bikes."

Chuck shrugged and rolled the toothpick around his mouth again. "Follow me. Watch your step."

Bicycle left the Fortune where it was. The scrapyard grounds were a maze of mess and weirdness. They threaded through rusted piles of machines and appliances whose useful life was behind them. Broken tennis rackets leaned against chipped garden gnomes. Some of the piles looked oddly artistic: a bedframe with four airplane propeller blades resting on it resembled four skinny people taking a nap; a tower of springs surrounded a barrel like a curly-haired head. They came to the shed with the grimy window that the Fortune had seen through the security cameras. Chuck undid its padlock.

The four Wheels of Fortune were huddled against one another in a corner behind a lawn mower. Bicycle had to stop herself from running over to hug them. "I need to check the derailleur limit screws," she said in a professional voice, making her way to the corner. She stroked the 713-A's frame, brushed away a bit of cobweb from the 713-B's frame, and rotated a pedal attached to the 713-C's frame. She murmured, "Help is here," to the 713-D's frame.

The 713-D faintly crooned, *"Thanks."*

Chuck lifted his head, so to cover for the bike Bicycle sang, "Thanks, thanks, thanks for showing these to me!" She then cleared her throat as she stood up and said, "Right, these look good. Please have them delivered at seven a.m. sharp tomorrow." She figured she could meet Chuck out front before her parents were awake and sneak the bikes into the commune's property room. Then she and her sisters could go "discover" them.

She and the Fortune made it back to Twintopia in twenty-two minutes, despite the uphill. There were times a person felt so good that even hill climbing couldn't slow them down.

Bicycle's good luck held all the way to the Kosroys' front door. Her sisters were standing in a cluster, arguing about whose turn it was to cycle. It looked like Daff had the helmet cam on, so Bicycle gave her a grinning thumbs-up.

"Oh, thank goodness you're back and you're fine and Mom and Dad didn't check on us so we didn't have to make anything up and no one is upset," said Cookie in a rush.

"We mostly scooted in slow motion. I tried some filming tricks to make it seem like each of us was at least two people," Daff said. "I'm interested to see how it came out."

"You accomplished what you wanted to," said Apple.

It wasn't a question, but Bicycle nodded anyway. "Tomorrow you'll have amazing bikes to ride that will fit you properly. No offense," she said to the too-small bike.

"*None taken.*" Cookie spoke for the bike in a voice

like that of Glinda the Good Witch. *"I am amazing in my own way."*

"Wait, we're getting those bikes? Those four-hundred-thousand-dollar bikes?" said Belladonna-Banana. "Did you rob a bank on your way to the scrapyard? You are even braver and more foolhardy than I thought."

"No bank robbing. The Fortune has some skills I'll tell you about another time," Bicycle said. "The main thing is that the bikes will be safe with us."

"Do they play music like yours?" asked Cookie.

"At least one of them does," said Bicycle. "I'm not exactly sure what features the bikes have in common with mine. They might have built-in tents, and the ability to create food, or know jokes that make sense."

"I hope mine can make candy bars," said Cookie.

"I hope mine has a graphing calculator," said Apple.

"I hope mine has a built-in camera," said Daff.

"I hope mine can tell jokes," said Belladonna-Banana. "No, that it can go underwater. No, that it can fold up small and fit in my pocket. Can I choose all of the above?"

When Sister Wanda called that evening, Bicycle didn't try to explain the situation with the Fortunes. The nun knew about the Fortune's money-printing ability and had given it a long lecture on how everyone, including bicycles, needed to behave as a decent member of society. She simply told the nun, "My sisters were great in their bike-riding lessons today."

"Wonderful," Sister Wanda said. "I can't imagine a better way for you to get to know each other."

"Me neither," Bicycle agreed. She felt her face wanting to frown and smile at the same time again. It was great that her sisters were excited about owning bikes. It was sad that they'd never get to ride them anywhere other than the hallway.

The next morning, Bicycle snuck extra-super-carefully out of bed slightly before seven a.m. Mom wasn't sleeping on their rug anymore. (Bicycle had been back nearly two weeks by now, and Mom seemed the teensiest bit more at ease.) She crept out of the apartment and met Chuck at the building's entrance. Chuck offloaded the bikes from the bed of his pickup truck in the dawn's early light.

Chuck slammed the tailgate closed. "Got that delivery fee for me?"

Bicycle handed him one twenty-dollar bill and one five, both freshly printed. She noticed he had another thick toothpick in his mouth. This one had the word UNIQUE burned into it.

"Pleasure doing business with you," he said. He drove his truck away in a fog of oily-smelling exhaust.

The bikes looked much happier out in the fresh air, even

though Chuck hadn't cleaned them off before delivering them. However, Bicycle couldn't dilly-dally outside too long, so she wheeled them one-by-one into the commune's property room, up close to the window where they could soak up some sun.

She compared the bikes' frames. They all looked similar to her Fortune, but 713-A had something that looked like a compass imbedded in its stem. Attached to the 713-B's handlebars was a purple orb with a round window cut into it, kind of like a Magic 8-Ball toy. The 713-C had a chunkier mountain-bike-esque frame, three water-bottle cages, and a front rack in addition to a rear rack. The 714-D had a prickle of plastic antenna things poking out from its front fork.

"So, hi," she said. "I'm Bicycle. You met me yesterday. I ride the Wheels of Fortune 713-J, who got your SOS message. You're safe now. You're going to meet your new riders a little later. I'm sure you'll get along." She debated for a moment telling the bikes that they'd be ridden only indoors from now on, and decided that could wait. "Do you have any questions?"

She waited but got no reaction. "It's a lot to take in. I know you're solar-powered, so I'll let you reenergize and be back as soon as I can. One sec—I do need to make you look like you've been here longer than a few minutes." She draped their seats and handlebars with random cables, doodads, and thingamabobs from the property room shelves. Then she ran back to the apartment, done with her last act of sneaki-ness, ready to be a model stay-close-to-home child.

When she crept in, the Fortune sparkled with green flashing lights to get her attention. How are they? Did you find out if they sent the original SOS message that brought us to Harpers Ferry?

"They're fine," she whispered. "They didn't tell me any-thing, but they may need more time to power up. You can ask them your questions later. I'm going to suggest we go search the property room again after everyone else is awake."

Let's wake them up now.

The Fortune promptly let out an enormous *YAWP* that did, indeed, wake up the rest of the family.

FAMILY REUNION #2

Bicycle apologized to their yawning faces. "I'm sorry my bike has problems." She gave it a disgruntled nudge. "But now that you're awake, do you want to go poke around the property room to see if we can find a few more bikes for riding practice?"

Her bleary-eyed parents informed her that there was plenty of time to prowl the property room after coffee, breakfast, and homeschooling lessons. Bicycle was able to wait, but the Fortune kept *bleep*ing and *bloop*ing to indicate its impatience. She would have sworn that it wriggled under her hands as she wheeled it down to the property room behind her family on the way to lunch. She'd told them she needed to bring the Fortune along so they could use it to measure the size of any bikes they found.

"Almost there," she murmured to it.

It blinked, I have never had a family reunion before.

In fact, I have never met other Wheels of Fortune before. I knew they existed, but they were not in the lab when Dr. Alvarado brought my programming online. Perhaps they will know where the models 713-E through 713-I ended up as well.

"What were the odds that both of our long-lost families would be in the same town at the same time?"

12,566,370 to 1. We are lucky.

Dad went into the property room first. He said, "Okay, everyone, look around, but I don't think—" He stopped dead when he saw the four bikes near the window. "How could I have missed those last time?"

Mom said, "Those look like good bikes. Are they?"

Bicycle pretended she was seeing them for the first time and removed the doodads and thingamabobs she'd used to camouflage them. She said, "These are top-of-the-line, the same brand as mine, see? And the perfect size, too."

"Well, who wants what?" Dad asked.

"This one is sophisticated," said Apple, claiming the 713-A.

"That one's got my name all over it," said Banana, pointing. "Well, if I decided that my name was the Wheels of Fortune 713-B. Which, just to be clear, I haven't."

"When Daff saw the four bikes on that fateful day, she knew which one was meant for her," murmured Daff, approaching the 713-D.

Cookie walked over to the 713-C and said shyly, "Hello, I'm Cookie."

Bicycle waited to see if the 713-C would do anything in response, but it stayed still and quiet, its computer screen blank.

"Okay, I guess I'm signing out four bikes," Dad said, scribbling details on a chart tacked to the back of the door. "I'll bring the smaller one back later this afternoon."

"Oh my," Mom said once they had them parked outside the cafeteria. "Are those lightning bolts on the frames? I bet these are racing bikes. They might go too fast."

"These are reliable bikes," Bicycle assured her, privately thinking there was no such thing as too fast. "They know how to take care of their riders."

A throng of boys on their way into the cafeteria did a double take at the five snazzy machines. "Hey, can I borrow one of those?" a boy asked.

Banana shooed them away. "Give us a chance to ride them first! Also, grow about four inches."

Another parent overheard Banana's comment and said something about how fast kids grow when you're not looking. Mom and Dad laughed and started talking with them about running out of right-sized clothes. While the parents conversed, Cookie jiggled the 713-C's frame and then did the same to the other bikes. "Why is my bike heavier than the others?" she asked Bicycle.

"I'm not sure," Bicycle said.

"What do these do?" asked Daff, plinking the metal whiskers jutting off her bike.

"Also not sure about that," Bicycle said.

"What is this?" Banana asked, tapping the purple orb on her handlebars. "A disco ball?"

Apple leaned over it and said, "If you look closely, you can see it has twelve sides. It's not a ball, it's a dodecahedron."

Banana retorted, "But what does it do, smarty-pants? None of the other bikes have one."

Apple shrugged.

Bicycle said, "I'll be honest—these probably have features that we'll only figure out once we start riding them. My bike still surprises me. I'm sure our practice this afternoon will be very interesting." She hoped none of these bikes had a missile launcher like the Fortune did, even though the projectiles it had launched in the past had been harmless. She was sure rubber snakes blasting into the air would not go over well with their parents.

On the way back to the apartment from lunch, Bicycle asked the Fortune, "Did you talk to the other bikes? What did you learn?"

I did not learn anything, the Fortune blinked. Their batteries are so drained that they need more than a dose of sunlight to get back online. Brisk pedaling will help kick-start the recharging process. They need a nice long ride outside.

"Urgh," Bicycle said. That was the one thing they weren't going to get. She hoped a ride several times around the hallway loop would do the trick. It'd be a shame to have rescued the bikes from melting only to consign them to a limbo with no energy to communicate.

Cycling practice that afternoon was fun. Apple, Banana, Cookie, and Daff were surprised at how much easier it was to ride a bigger bike than the little one they'd been using. Unfortunately, the 713s (A, B, C, and D) acted like perfectly ordinary bikes the whole time. Even after three times around the loop, no words, music, food pellets, or missiles popped out from any unexpected orifices.

"My do-dekka-disco-ball wobbles a little," Banana told Bicycle. "Look!" She tapped it like a bongo drum. It did indeed wobble.

"Be careful—I bet it does more than that," Bicycle told her.

They need a nice long ride outside, the Fortune blinked again. It is like they are in a coma. Please eat a candy bar and cheer me up.

"Maybe my sisters will cover for me so I can take each bike outside to wake them up," Bicycle said. She didn't want to put her sisters in a difficult position again, facing a potential Mom-and-Dad worry-explosion, but there didn't seem to be any other options.

She explained the situation and asked if they'd cover for her a few more times. Apple shook her head no.

Bicycle sighed. "Okay." The Fortune's siblings would stay unconscious for who knew how long, but at least they weren't melted into metal goo.

Then Apple said, "You don't understand. We don't want you to take our bikes for a ride. We want to do what you did—sneak away during cycling practice to have an adventure. You'll help us, won't you?"

A GLUG OF INDEPENDENCE

Bicycle's first thought was *I'm twisting myself up like a pretzel to fit in, and you want my help to break free?* Her second thought was *I'm a bad influence. My sisters had a happy life, never knowing any different. Then I came along and—bam!—they think it's time to cycle headfirst into the unknown. I'm turning my family upside down.*

Apple seemed to pluck part of this second thought right out of her brain. "You aren't a bad influence. This isn't the first time we've talked about doing something like this. We thought we could wait until we turned eighteen, but when we heard about the adventures you had this summer, and saw how you slipped away and came back without Mom and Dad having to freak out . . . Well, we don't want to wait anymore."

Banana and Daff were nodding.

Cookie lowered her eyes to her sneakers.

Bicycle asked her, "You feel the same way?"

Cookie said, "I don't need an adventure. I'll help everyone else have theirs."

"You're not fooling anyone, you know," said Banana. "Quint Sense rats you out. You want to go enter that eating contest. Especially because you found out the next food is pie."

Cookie groaned. "If we mess up, Mom's going to make a way worse face than the one like she's peeling a stuck Band-Aid off her heart. No amount of pie would be worth that."

"We saw that they don't worry if they don't know there's anything to worry about," Banana said.

"We don't want to hide stuff from them," Daff said. "We thought we could each take a turn, and then tell Mom and Dad all the great things we enjoyed once we were done. Apple thinks they'll be impressed by how happy we are, and that'll show them we can start having more independence."

Bicycle said, "Let me get this straight. One of you goes to do something fun while the rest of us cover for her. After everyone does the fun things and nothing bad happens, we tell Mom and Dad. Then we hope that it convinces them we should start living differently."

They nodded.

Apple said, "It's like Mom and Dad are frozen. Waiting for them to thaw on their own isn't happening."

"This would be our way of giving them a warm nudge," Banana said.

"Of course, there's a chance it'll make things worse," said Daff.

"A big chance," said Cookie.

Apple said, "But there's a chance it might make things better. And I'd get to walk a *dog*. Please say you've got our backs. Sisters help sisters."

For guidance, Bicycle quickly reviewed the three Rules of Family Belonging: Find a Place to Fit In, Ask Before You Use the Bathroom, and Be Whoever They Need You to Be, Even If It's Someone You're Not. As far as she could tell, her sisters needed her to be the opposite person that her parents needed her to be. Family life was complicated.

"Can you calculate how likely it is that my sisters' plan is going to work out well?" she asked the Fortune.

Chances are 98% that it will work out well for the Fortunes. They will wake up from their comas if they go on an adventure longer than a mile away.

"That's not what I meant," Bicycle explained.

I know. The odds in your sisters' favor are not as high.

There was no clear right answer. It looked like Bicycle had to choose a side: squish her true self down to be the best daughter, or let her true self free to be the best sister.

The part she'd been squishing since she'd gotten to Twintopia spoke up. "Who is going first?" she said.

"Me!" said Daff. "The Halloween Horror Movie Festival is Saturday. Do you think you can coach me to be ready by then? I don't care what movie I go to—I'd be happy to see basically anything."

Daff was making great progress, but she'd only been riding for three days. Bicycle asked, "Where is the movie festival?"

Daff described the location of the movie house, and the Fortune mapped it out. It wasn't far, but there was no way to get there that didn't involve riding on roads, most of which had no sidewalks.

"I hate to say this, but you're not ready for riding down a road by yourself," Bicycle said. "There's a lot to know about traffic rules and how to stay safe."

Daff looked crestfallen.

"If I could go with you, that would help," Bicycle said. "My bike could even look out for your bike. But then there would be only three of you to pretend to be five of us. Is that even possible?"

"Oh! I could show you three how to aim the helmet cam to make it seem like a lot is going on," said Daff. "It's worth a try, isn't it?"

"I've got enough personality for at least two people," said Banana. "Wait, I still get to play myself, right?"

"Who else could handle it?" said Apple. "Come on, let's try it out right now. Bicycle and Daff, go do a road-rules lesson down that hallway"—she pointed down a hall running per- pendicular to their own—"and the other three of us will try to be extra . . . lively. I'll wear the helmet cam. We can see if Mom and Dad come out to check what's going on; if they do, it's easy enough to say you made a wrong turn and get you back."

They tried it. Mom and Dad did not come out into the hallway. When practice was over, they tried wheeling all of the bikes into the apartment, but it quickly became clear that there wasn't room for more than Bicycle's Fortune. They leaned them in a huddle against the outside lockers, where Cookie taped up a sign that said PLEASE ASK THE KOSROYS BEFORE BORROWING.

Back inside, Banana asked Mom and Dad, "So, what did you think of our riding today? Did you notice how full of personality Daff and then Bicycle looked out there?"

Apple surreptitiously smacked Banana's elbow.

"It looked like you were busy out there!" Mom said. "The camera was swooshing all over the place. Those new bikes didn't make you ride faster than you were comfortable going, did they?"

"No," said Daff. "I feel way more confident now. Did you know you always ride on the right side of a road or path and walk on the left side? 'Ride right,' Bicycle told me to commit to memory."

Banana said, "Our new bikes are empowering. I feel like I'm twice the girl I used to be. Maybe even three times."

Apple smacked Banana's other elbow.

"I'm impressed with you girls," Dad said.

163

That night, the Fortune got Bicycle's attention before she went to bed. Your sisters are ready to try adventures for the first time. Are you ready to have them again?

"Going to the movies is such a small thing. I don't know if I'd even classify it as an adventure."

One can rarely be sure about how an adventure of any size will unfold. You cannot have forgotten the unpredictability of the open road, **the Fortune blinked.** Do you remember when traveling west you got caught in a storm in Colorado and had to spend the night in a ghost town? And in the same location traveling back east, you went to help an armadillo cross the street and it did not want your help?

Bicycle shuddered. The ghost town had been spooky and that armadillo had been ornery. "But this isn't a cross-country marathon, it's a mile and a half to a movie theater. How much could go wrong?"

72.6% of people who have said that statement then had things go wrong.

"Why are you trying to talk me out of this? And how could you know that?"

I know 77.3% of the things there are to know. Also, I am not trying to talk you out of it. The 713-D needs to go for a ride. So does your sister. I want to help you be aware of what you are getting yourself into.

"Did you know you sometimes sound like Sister Wanda? I'm as aware as I need to be," Bicycle said. She knew that sometimes you had to move forward, even not knowing exactly what lay in front of you.

Saturday, two days later, was Halloween. The tradition for the day at Twintopia was that the littlest littles came around in costumes to each apartment with their parents to trick-or-treat between one and two o'clock, while the older kids made the rounds after dinner. Bicycle and her sisters had decided they'd go as simple versions of the five senses— Apple was Hearing, with big fake ears and a little portable radio; Banana was Touch, with boxing gloves; Cookie was Smell, with a Pinocchio nose and a pumpkin spice candle; Daff was Sight, with glasses that had huge bouncing eyeballs attached to them; and Bicycle was Taste, with a picture of a mouth with a tongue sticking out pinned to her shirt.

Answering the door to itty-bitty trick-or-treaters and their parents turned out to be highly entertaining. Some of the littlest little kids would stand at the door, mystified as to what they were supposed to do. Others would try to give the Kosroys candy instead of taking it from them. A few yelled "Treat!" and held out their hands with a smile. One little boy was dressed in white with black spots and had a bell around his neck. Bicycle asked, "What are you?"

The boy told her, "I'm a cow! Oink!"

"Works for me," she said, and dropped a packet of Skittles into his sack.

Bicycle saw a lot of the families she'd gotten to know at mealtimes, but not the Lakshmis. She asked if they'd be stopping by, and Mom said, "Oh, no! Trick-or-treating with multiple six-month-olds is pointless torture for all involved. I'll be sure to drop off a nice pile of candy for Mr. and Mrs. Lakshmi later."

Finally, the commune's littles were finished trick-or-treating and the girls could start their cycling practice. Bicycle and Daff quickly removed their costumes and hid them in a hallway locker so that Apple, Banana, and Cookie could take turns putting them on for acting purposes. They synchronized their watches, and Bicycle and Daff vowed they'd be back by six at the latest.

"Please be careful," said Cookie.

"We're all rooting for you," said Apple.

"Don't screw this up for the rest of us, okay?" said Banana.

Daff saluted them. "Thanks for letting me go first." She turned to Bicycle. "Ready when you are."

"Follow me, do what I do, and let me know the minute your bike starts talking, or glowing, or behaving in any way you don't expect a bike to behave," Bicycle told her. "Here we go."

CELEBRATE GOOD TIMES

It was a crisp October afternoon, a fine day to pedal out into the world. Bicycle didn't do what her body's instincts told her to do—*zoom!*—but instead put on her brakes and went at sloth speed. She glanced over her shoulder every few seconds, wishing she had another set of eyes in the back of her head so she could both watch where she was going and make sure Daff wasn't having any problems.

Daff asked, "Should I keep looking over my shoulder, too? That wasn't something you taught us during cycling practice."

"No," Bicycle called back to her. "Do what I do except for that." Looking backward was a sure way for a new cyclist to swerve into traffic. "I want to make sure I don't leave you behind."

"I promise to yell 'Hey!' if you're getting too far ahead of me. In fact, you could go faster, you know. I keep having to put on my brakes."

Bicycle smiled and sped up a fraction to zooming sloth speed. She then heard Daff speaking to herself. ("The air was cool and smelled smoky on the first day I ever rode a bike outside. . . .") Daff continued narrating everything she saw and felt and thought. Bicycle stopped trying to grow back-of-the-head eyeballs—as long as Daff was talking about the color of the leaves and the sound of tires whirring over pavement, she knew her newbie cycling sister was okay.

They arrived at the Harpers Ferry Movie House without even the whisper of a problem. The movie marquee said HALLOWEEN HORROR MOVIE FESTIVAL—WELCOME TO THE FRIGHT FEST. There were black-and-white posters with zombies, werewolves, giant spiders, and a mesmerizing Dracula in a tuxedo with a cape.

"We made it!" Daff raised her arms and bowed to the posters. "Moviemakers, I am here to learn." Then she turned and bowed to Bicycle. "Thank you so much for bringing me here."

"You're welcome, but don't forget you brought yourself here. I officially proclaim you a cyclist. I just need to check something." Bicycle asked the 713-D, "Hello? How are you feeling?"

It made a *meep* noise.

"Aw!" said Daff, and patted it.

"Was that a good *meep*?" Bicycle asked the Fortune.

The Fortune blinked, Yes. Its reboot has begun.

Daff checked the list of films that were playing and their start times. She said, "Can we go inside? The next movie up should be *The Revenge of Frankenstein*, and I don't want to miss the opening sequence."

Bicycle hesitated, and the Fortune told her, We will sit in the sunshine and I will monitor the 713-D's progress. You may go watch Frankenstein have his revenge.

Daff used her allowance money to pay for their tickets and a satisfyingly large bag of popcorn from the concession stand. Daff and Bicycle entered the theater just as the lights were dimming and the sound of a bell tolling came from the sound system. The opening sequence was pretty grim, with Dr. Frankenstein being led to the guillotine. The popcorn was good, though—it had real melted butter on it.

Daff started off muttering notes to herself but ended up so entranced by the movie she became silent. They watched as Dr. Frankenstein faked his own death and then transplanted the brain of his assistant, Karl, into a new body. Naturally, things went wrong from there. The plot unfolded gradually. At first, there weren't many jump-scare surprises that startled Bicycle. That changed about halfway through the movie.

Wha-hoo! Jubilant dance music resounded over the scene of Karl cramming his old body into a furnace. The whole theater jumped in shock. Popcorn pieces flew everywhere. Then the band Kool and the Gang crooned over the speakers about celebrating good times together.

"What is that?" theatergoers yelled. "Boooo! You mixed up the soundtrack!"

A bunch of folks craned their necks toward the back of the theater, so Bicycle did, too. She saw the shadow of someone dashing back and forth in the projector room. The music continued as if a wedding reception were in full swing. She turned back to face the screen, where Karl was running amok and not bringing any good times to anyone.

The film slowed and stopped. A voice came over the loudspeaker: "So sorry, film fans, we are experiencing technical difficulties. Our sound system appears to have been hacked. Let me see if this will work . . ." Now soul music poured out over the audience, James Brown letting the world know that he felt good, so good.

Bicycle squirmed, dumping some kernels of popcorn onto her lap. This unexpected music burst resembled what the Fortune had been doing. She scooped up the kernels, hoping with all her hoping powers that the music mix-up wasn't the fault of hers or Daff's bikes.

The film stopped again. The voice explained, "I am turning off the speakers while we work this out. In the meantime, please enjoy *The Revenge of Frankenstein* as a silent movie. Thank you for your patience." The film restarted without any music or voices. Onscreen, Karl started losing control of his own body, looking tortured.

The theater was silent while the movie watchers assessed this new turn of events. It didn't take long for some of them to pass judgment.

"Boooo! This is no good! I want my money back!"

"Wait!" shouted someone who stood up in the front row. "I am a big fan of this movie, and I know it all by heart. I can recite the dialogue if you'll be quiet." People settled down to give the big fan a chance. He started doing Dr. Frankenstein's voice and turned out to have talent. He gave Karl a growly gargle of a voice that was more spooky than the real actor's, and also did a believable falsetto for the leading lady's lines. Bicycle stole a glance at Daff, hoping she was still having fun. She was frowning.

"He's not doing the sound effects," she whispered to Bicycle. "Or the tension-building background music. It's like half the movie without those."

A person behind them overhead Daff and said, "That's true." They shouted to the rest of the audience, "Who's got loud shoes? Stomp your feet to make footstep sounds when a character walks. Whoever's got a rasping voice, make a creaky noise when a door opens."

"I can do the wind," someone yelled back.

"I can sing eerie music. *Deedly deedly deedly whooOOO!*" came another voice. "Who will help me do that?"

At first, there was nothing more than a few half-hearted

footsteps and a couple of *whooOOOs*. Then someone mimicked an excellent *eeeeek* door creak, and folks tittered and applauded them.

At that point, the audience really got into making a live-action soundtrack. A whole section of the theater took it upon themselves to hum dramatically. Some people started improvising, adding the sounds of neighing horses and clattering carriage wheels, then frogs croaking and crows cawing even when the action was taking place inside. Things went from interesting to noisy. Bicycle glanced at Daff to see what she wanted to do. Stay? Go? Daff wasn't participating in the sounds, nor was she narrating what was going on, but she stayed put.

They watched through to the end when Dr. Frankenstein's own brain gets placed into a new body. The manager gave each person exiting the theater a free ticket to come back and see something else. Daff rubbed her ticket between two fingers and said, "It'd be nice to see another movie in a normal way. I had this idea in my mind I'd absorb inspiration from the movie. Instead, it was . . . what it was." She sighed as they went to get their bikes.

Bicycle didn't really want to know if the Fortune had been the one to ruin the movie, but she asked it anyway as they started to pedal. "Did you happen to try to . . . communicate with us during the movie?"

I did not. The 713-D did. Once its reboot was complete,

it wanted to let Daff know how happy and grateful it was. It has the same music database that I do, plus broadcasting antenna with a wide range. It was the one who sent us all the SOS messages.

"Were my sisters right when they guessed why the SOS signals were so short and far between—was it because the 713-D got stuck in that shed where it could barely recharge itself when it rained so much?"

Yes.

Bicycle whispered, "Yay that it's rebooted, but the noise kind of ruined the show." She decided she wasn't going to tell Daff that her new bike had wrecked her first-ever adventure. However, the 713-D broke the news itself. It chose this moment to blast Kool and the Gang's "Celebrate" from its own speakers.

Daff wobbled in surprise. "Too loud!" she said. The 713-D immediately turned down the volume. "Why is my bike doing this? Did I get a musical bike like yours? Wait—why is it playing the same music that interrupted the movie?"

Bicycle tried to smooth things over. "My bike says your bike wanted to share how happy it was to be fully functional again. It sent the music into the theater to, um, thank you for riding it." She hoped Daff wouldn't be too angry.

Daff mulled this over as they started up a hill. She finally said to the 713-D, "I'm glad you're working right again. You are fun to ride. But let me tell you why I don't want you to play more music during movies." She explained how much she'd looked forward to seeing a movie the way it was meant to be seen. The 713-D played cheesy horror soundtrack music in response, then something with lyrics about being sorry, so sorry. Bicycle knew it felt bad for ruining the movie and hoped it had learned its lesson about broadcasting musical messages into unfamiliar situations.

Daff then asked her bike, "Do you at least have a built-in camera?"

The 713-D sang the word *No* and a jazzy phrase about how it had got just about everything.

Bicycle asked the Fortune, "Does the 713-D speak only through songs?"

Yes. Dr. Alvarado programmed it to communicate through music rather than written messages.

"That's too bad," Bicycle said. It seemed like a lot of potential for headaches. "Did you find out where these bikes were before they came to the scrapyard, and where the other 713 models might be?"

These four bikes were originally picked up by the U.S. government from Dr. Alvarado to be tested for their value to the military. They languished in a warehouse until being sold online. Whoever bought them must have taken them to the scrapyard. Unfortunately, they have no data on the whereabouts of the models built between us.

Dusk was approaching, and although both bikes had

bright front and rear lights, Bicycle pushed Daff to ride with urgency. When they got inside Twintopia, they sped through the hallways, skidding to a halt by their front door in time to see Mom's head pop out. "There you are!" she said.

"Yes!" Bicycle said, her shoulders up around her ears. She was too flustered to read her mom's expression—was she about to explode and ground the quintuplets forever?

"Can you wrap things up so we can head to dinner? I've been tempted to eat the bags of trick-or-treating candy," Mom said.

"Tempted?" Dad's head joined Mom's. "The pile of Skittles wrappers next to the computer says you were more than tempted."

Mom clucked at him and said to Bicycle, "Are your sisters right behind you? It's dinnertime, period. Oh good, there they are."

Apple, Banana, and Cookie coasted up, looking beat.

"We're going to eat now. No more of this 'one more time around the bend' stuff. After that, you can go trick-or-treating." She didn't seem to notice that Apple was wearing Bicycle's costume tongue shirt with her fake ears, or that Banana had both boxing gloves and goggles with springy eyeballs.

"Quick bathroom break and we're right behind you," Apple said, nudging Bicycle. The girls abandoned their bikes and crowded into the bathroom. Banana slid to the tiled floor as soon as the door was closed.

"Was it worth it?" Banana asked Daff, and immediately cut her off. "No, the answer is no, because being more than me for almost two hours is too much."

"Mom came out to ask us questions three times," said Apple, running her fingers through her hair so it stood out around her face like a dark lion's mane. "We made Cookie do the talking because she was being herself most of the time, but it was stressful."

Cookie's eyes were intense as she said, "It felt like walking a tightrope."

Banana said, "It felt like riding a tightrope on a unicycle is what it felt like. What if we'd gotten found out? Then I'd never get my chance to go be amazing at karate, which I am doing tomorrow, and no one is arguing with me about whose turn it is next."

Apple kicked Banana's feet. "You can't both say it isn't worth it and then say you're going next."

"Of course I can, I just did," said Banana.

Daff cut in. "It wasn't like I thought it would be, but maybe you'll have better luck than I did. It wouldn't be fair to give up until we all get a chance."

"Only if who goes next gets decided with rock-paper-scissors," said Apple, jabbing her finger at Banana.

Everyone agreed. Banana won all four rounds of rock-paper-scissors without breaking a sweat.

REAP THE WHIRLWIND

"I'm good, I'm set," Banana insisted the next afternoon when they gathered in the hallway. "I don't need Bicycle to come with me. I mean, how hard could this be? I have natural cycling talent."

The Fortune blinked, 69.6% of people who ask "How hard could it be?" provoke a change in their luck.

"A change for better or worse?" Bicycle asked.

Yes, one of those, the Fortune answered.

The other girls tried to convince Banana to practice riding a few more days before setting out on her lone adventure, but she was adamant that she was going right away. "Today is Sunday, and the ad on the public bulletin board at the convenience store says that Milosz Martial Arts offers free introductory karate classes on Sundays."

"Do you know which side of the road you're supposed to stay on?" Daff challenged her.

"The right side," Banana said breezily. "Ride right, walk left. I heard you reciting that when Bicycle taught you the rules of the road."

"How do you know where the martial arts place is?" Apple asked.

"I asked Bicycle's bicycle. It printed me a map. And I borrowed one of Cookie's sweatshirts so I can carry it." Banana patted her hoodie sweatshirt's pocket. "Look—I'm wearing my shin guards, my elbow pads, and my helmet. Nobody needs to worry about me. And things will be easier for you if Bicycle stays—four pretending to be five has got to be easier than three. Even I know the math for that checks out."

Cookie's forehead was furrowed. "I don't like the idea of you out there alone." She hunted around in her own pockets and pulled out a tangerine. "Take this. And"—she hunted some more—"this." She gave Banana a box of raisins. "Can't you convince her that she needs you?" Cookie asked Bicycle.

Bicycle was examining the twelve-sided object on the 713-B's handlebars. The window cut into the object was dark. There was no telling what might be inside. She said to Banana, "This whatsis could be anything." (Only Apple could remember its correct name, so the rest of them called it a "whatsis.") "When your bike's power comes on, this might start communicating with the international space station, or shooting rubber snakes at pedestrians, or putting out a frequency that calls an army of bats or something."

"How did I never know bikes could be this cool? But enough talking! I'm wasting valuable karate time." Banana got on her bike and started pedaling. "When I get back with my army of bats, you must start addressing me as Batgirl."

Apple made a frustrated noise as they watched her go. "We can't let her do this alone," she said.

"We won't," said Bicycle. "I'll follow her. Sisters have each other's backs, right?" She couldn't be annoyed with Banana. She knew what it felt like to be impatient to go and full of confidence that things wouldn't be that hard. But she also knew that confidence would only take you so far. "I'm sorry to leave you here to pretend to be me again."

"Just hope Mom and Dad don't come talk to us like yesterday," Apple said.

"I picked out their favorites from our Halloween candy and left a pile next to the computer," said Cookie. "I thought it might keep them extra-interested in staying put."

"Good thinking," said Daff. She told Bicycle, "Go after Batgirl. Just in case this happened, I wrote a script on how the three of us would act like the five of us. How hard could it be to do that?"

"I'm going," said Bicycle. "But let's stop using the question 'How hard could it be?' for now."

Banana was farther ahead than Bicycle expected her to be.

She does have natural cycling talent, the Fortune

observed. She has the makings of a racer. She is fearless about her speed.

Bicycle could tell from her sister's posture that she was drinking in the delight of moving fast under her own power. She thought about her bike-racing friend Zbig, who on their trip across the country had told her, "The fastest cyclists are able to turn off the parts of their brain that know we have no wings. When we are pushing toward the finish line, we tell ourselves we can fly."

Bicycle was glad Mom and Dad couldn't see their two girls right now, both flying down the street.

She nearly caught up to her sister but stayed behind her and didn't call out, not wanting to startle her. When Banana made an abrupt turn onto a dirt driveway, Bicycle followed.

This is the wrong way, the Fortune informed her. The map I printed shows the martial arts studio farther down the street.

Neither of them could go very fast on the bumpy driveway, so Bicycle decided this would be a good time to get Banana's attention. "Hello!" she called out.

Banana twisted her head around, hit a rock, and tipped over. The shin guards and elbow pads did their job, and she was already brushing herself off by the time Bicycle caught up and asked if she was all right.

"That was my first fall of the whole ride, so I'm pretty good, I'd say," Banana told her. "You came after me, huh?"

"Yeah. It was the sisterly thing to do," Bicycle said. "You turned the wrong way back there, so you may want to check your map."

"I was just doing what my bike's whatsis told me to do," Banana said. Bicycle saw its window was glowing with a pale purple light and showed the words **TURN RIGHT** in dark violet letters.

"It's waking up, that's great." Bicycle chewed her bottom lip. "But if it's giving you bad directions, that's less great. Fortune, do you think its energy is too low or out of whack?"

We don't make mistakes when it comes to directions. Did Banana tell it where she wanted to go?

Bicycle relayed the question, and Banana said, "All I said was I was excited to meet a real martial arts teacher. Oh my goodness, look at the cute goose. Hi, goosey!"

A big gray goose was waddling up to them, its head snaking from side to side. It seemed to be in a hurry, reminding Bicycle of the rabbit from *Alice in Wonderland* who was late for a very important date. It stopped reminding Bicycle of the rabbit, however, when it opened up its orange beak and hissed like a furious tea kettle.

Banana had been moving toward it. She stopped. "Whoa, goosey, we're friendly."

That goose may be defending its territory. Hold your bikes in front of you. We can withstand pecking that you may find painful.

"Let's get behind our bikes!" Bicycle yelled. They did this none too soon. The goose stamped its feet, hissed louder, and then proceeded to peck the 713-B's front wheel with manic abandon. Bicycle tried to remember if birds had teeth, because this one looked determined to rip the tire off the bike. Toothless or not, it somehow managed to make a puncture. The bike tire let out its own hiss as air started escaping. This *ssss* seemed to enrage the goose. It redoubled its efforts to destroy.

"What do we do now?" Banana said. The whatsis on the 713-B glowed with a new message: AT THIS TIME, A SNACK WOULD BE A GOOD IDEA.

"For us, or for the goose?" Banana asked it. "Never mind." She pulled the tangerine out of her pocket and gave it to Bicycle, then took out the box of raisins. "I don't know what calms the heart of vicious creatures better, so let's try both." Bicycle tore off a piece of the tangerine's skin, and the tangy smell got the goose's attention. It stopped pecking and lifted its head toward Bicycle.

"See this yummy-yum here," she said in a singsong voice. "Much better than rubber bike tires." She peeled off a section and tossed it behind the goose. "Go get it!"

The goose watched the tangerine slice arc through the air and plop on the ground. It turned back to the girls and squinted in a way that made Bicycle think of the actor Clint Eastwood letting someone know that this town wasn't big enough for the both of them.

Banana ripped open the box of raisins and shook some into her hand. "How about some of nature's candy instead?" She tossed the black nuggets in the same direction as the tangerine slice.

The goose watched the raisins hit the ground with quiet seriousness. It started swaying its neck back and forth as if it planned to hypnotize the raisins before eating them.

"Nope, no raisins for geese!" someone yelled from the house. A young man dressed in spandex exercise clothes pushed open a screen door. "Didn't you see the sign that says PLEASE DON'T FEED THE GOOSE? He's on a diet."

Bicycle and Banana looked around for the sign. Banana saw it first, near a chicken coop, and pointed it out to the young man. It had been pulled down into a mud puddle and had webbed footprints on it.

The goose started to run for the raisins. The young man saw him go and dashed out the door. The man got to the raisins first, standing atop them while the goose hissed at his sneakers.

"Goose Lee is having difficulty curbing his appetite," the man said.

"Ha!" said Banana. "His name sounds like Bruce Lee, the kung fu master."

"That's because Goose Lee is named after the great and honorable Master Bruce, may he never be forgotten," the man told them. "I bought this goose to help protect my flock of chickens by chasing off predators. Then I noticed he had serious kung fu skills. I studied with the Shaolin monks in China after college, so I know serious kung fu skills when I see them. Watch Goose Lee's lightning speed." The man arranged himself into a fighting stance, raising his fists to chest height and planting one foot back. He accidentally uncovered a few of the raisins. The goose didn't waste a millisecond. He drove his beak into the dirt to nab the tiny treats, tossing them back into its gullet. He gulped, dipped his head, and made a rapid-fire honking sound like he was laughing at the man.

The man shook a finger. "You know it isn't good for you to snack between meals."

"Sir, we're sorry we fed your goose by mistake. We'll get out of here so I can go to Milosz Martial Arts for my free class," said Banana.

"You want to learn martial arts? Forget that place, it's a rip-off. What you want to do is spend some time with Goose Lee. You've heard of the animal fighting styles of the Shaolin monks?"

Banana shook her head.

"Fighters learn to embody aspects of the tiger, the crane, the dragon, the praying mantis, stuff like that. Goose Lee here leaves those other critters in the dust. He's fast, sneaky, powerful, bold, and unpredictable. He can confuse his opponents with sudden cuteness. Legend has it that Bruce Lee developed Jeet Kune Do by hanging out with a flock of particularly aggressive geese in Hong Kong."

No legend says that about Bruce Lee, the Fortune told Bicycle. Here is a patch for the 713-B's flat tire. It produced a glue-on patch.

Bicycle told the man, "We'll leave your driveway, I just need a few minutes to fix the tire that Goose Lee attacked."

"Oy," the man said. "I've been trying to teach him that bikes aren't a threat. If it makes you feel any better, he attacks cars the same way. I've seen him flatten a semitrailer tire."

"What's his best move?" Banana asked as Bicycle got busy removing the 713-B's wheel. "He doesn't do kicks, does he?"

"Of course he does. Flying kicks. But his best move is called Reap the Whirlwind. Goose Lee! Do your whirlwind!"

Goose Lee just glared single-mindedly at the man's feet.

"Can you distract him for a minute while I scoop up the rest of the raisins?"

Banana was game. "Here, Goose Lee!" She waved the box of raisins. "These are nicer, no dirt on them!"

The goose snapped his head around and zeroed in on the box. He took a couple of waddling steps forward.

" 'Be water, my friend'—that's a quote from Bruce Lee himself," Banana told him.

The goose raised its wings as far up as they could stretch

and ran at Banana, beak open, flapping and hissing like he'd swallowed a hundred rattlesnakes. Banana screamed and ran away.

"That's Reap the Whirlwind," said the man, picking up the raisins. "Good distraction, thanks."

The goose continued to chase Banana around the yard.

"Don't run!" the man said. "It makes you look like prey."

"Can't you call him off?" Banana yelled back, continuing to sprint.

"Goose Lee has issues with authority," the man said.

The 713-B glowed with the words SEEK SHELTER.

"Get over here!" Bicycle told Banana, who dived behind the bikes. Bicycle held the loose wheel up in front of them like a shield.

Banana asked her bike, "Can you summon that army of bats now? Or the international space station?"

YOUR LUCK IS ABOUT TO CHANGE, the 713-B's whatsis advised.

Bicycle was wondering which way their luck would be changing—for better or worse—when Goose Lee pecked their tire shield.

"Stop! Pecking! My! Bike!" Banana howled. She stood on her tiptoes and raised her hands above her head, mimicking the goose's body language. She started flapping her arms and let out a vicious snake-swallowing hiss of her own.

The goose drew his neck back and paused. His bitey

little brain contemplated Banana's wild flap-hissings. Then he silently bowed his head and waddled away.

"Told you," the man said. "Goose Lee can teach you all the moves you need. Hey, don't go in there!"

The goose had gotten up on the porch and was using its beak to prod open the screen door. He managed to slither through the slim wedge of an opening, and the man bolted after him.

"Come back anytime for another self-defense lesson," he said over his shoulder.

"Yeah, right," said Bicycle. "Come on, we'll fix the tire down near the road." She and Banana got themselves and the Fortunes out of there. By the time the flat was fixed and they'd ridden to Milosz Martial Arts, the door was locked and the lights were off.

"Can't believe I missed having a real karate class because of an attack goose," Banana said morosely. "Should we just go home now or what?"

The 713-B's whatsis glowed. AT THIS TIME, A SNACK WOULD BE A GOOD IDEA.

"This doesn't just *look* like a Magic 8-Ball—I think it *acts* like one, too," Banana said. "It has preset sayings that show up for different occasions. Let's see if it can answer questions like your Fortune can. Can you go underwater?" she asked it.

YES, INDEED.

"Can you fold up small and fit in my pocket?"

NO, NOT AT ALL.

"Can you tell knock-knock jokes?"

AT THIS TIME, A SNACK WOULD BE A GOOD IDEA.

"So far, that is my favorite saying."

The Fortune told them, Our inventor experimented with different methods of communication. He was likely inspired by the Mostly Silent Monks, whom he admired, to create a bike that communicates everything necessary through a few set phrases.

Banana read its screen and said, "The Mostly Silent Monks, huh? Aren't they the folks you grew up with?"

"I grew up with the Mostly Silent Monks in Washington, D.C.," said Bicycle, "but there are Mostly Silent Monasteries across the country. The Mostly Silent order is pretty famous, since they are great listeners."

"I'd like to go to visit one someday. I'd like to do a lot of things someday." Banana tilted her head to the side and contemplated the 713-B. "For now, we make the best of things. We snack."

Banana pulled out the remaining raisins and split them with Bicycle. Bicycle started to nibble, while Banana threw her entire handful of raisins into her mouth at once. She snaked her head back and forth and imitated Goose Lee's rapid-fire honking sound, which made her choke and cough. Bicycle pounded her on the back until she was able to swallow.

"I'm sorry things didn't go the way you planned," Bicycle said. She tried to think of something that might help salvage the experience. "Do you want to lead the way home? You can go as fast as you want."

Banana's face lit up. She asked her bike "What do you say? Do you feel the need for speed?"

The whatsis glowed. YES, INDEED.

WALK A DOG OR BIKE A CAT

Banana and Bicycle got back early. Their sisters still looked worn out, but less so than the day before.

Cookie said, "Daff's script made things easier. It told us when to change personalities and where to point the camera. Her bike played background music."

Apple said, "Mom and Dad poked their heads out of the door only once today. Luckily, Daff's bike played this song—'When the Moon Comes Over the Mountain'—that turned out to be from their wedding, so it distracted them into going back inside to smooch. They might be getting used to the idea of their offspring doing things without them. I think our plan of having these adventures and then telling them later that they went well is going to work."

"I wouldn't exactly say my ride went well," Banana said. "We took a wrong turn, and I missed karate class. Although I guess I did learn one move." She raised her arms above her head and flapped them, hissing and running at Daff, who screamed and ducked behind Apple. "That's called Reap the Whirlwind. It's kind of terrifying, isn't it? Maybe it'll be my secret weapon."

"I thought you had a map," Cookie said. "How did you take a wrong turn?"

Banana answered, "My bike's whatsis glowed purple and told me to go a different way." She frowned at the 713-B and asked it, "Why did you tell me to turn down that driveway?"

It lit up. IT IS NEVER WRONG TO LEND A HELPING HAND.

"Hmm." Banana looked at Bicycle. "We can trust these things, can't we? Would they send us off on a wild-goose chase? Ha! Get it?"

"No, I'm sure the 713-B just wants to help," Bicycle told her. "It must have made a mistake." She didn't feel great, though, that two of her sisters' adventures had been derailed by the Fortunes' behavior.

Apple said, "Let's not do any more adventures for a few days, then. Cookie and I can plan out every last detail of what we want to do so that nothing will go wrong for us." She raised her eyebrows at Cookie.

Cookie waggled her head. "I know I'm not ready."

Bicycle decided she wanted to be more ready as well. She made a mental note to ask the Fortune to mind-meld with the 713-D and 713-B and see if they could warn Apple and

Cookie about any unusual characteristics of the 713-A and 713-C.

Apple's decision to proceed slowly and cautiously went out the window that night when the family watched the evening news on television. In a segment called "Furry Friends," a reporter arrived at the animal shelter to pretend to interview dogs and cats who needed adopting. All the animals looked nice and hopeful, except one creature described as a "spirit cat" who hid under a towel and refused to come out. The last dog on camera was called Nugget, and his appearance made Apple slide off the couch onto her knees.

"This puppy just arrived today, and he won't be here long," the shelter manager said, holding the black-eyed ball of white fluff in her lap. "Nugget appears to be part Samoyed, which is a breed of dog that likes cold weather. They're nicknamed 'smiling dogs' because their faces always look like they're happy to see you."

The reporter asked Nugget, "Are you, in fact, happy to see us?" and held the microphone up to the little dog's nose. Nugget grinned at the camera with his mouth open, exposing a pink tongue.

"Ohhh," said Apple, reaching out to the screen with one hand.

"He is adorable," Mom said, stroking the scar on her chin. "But you just never know with dogs."

Apple put her hand down and slumped.

Later, when they were all in bed, Apple said into the darkness, "I need to talk to all of you about biking practice tomorrow."

"No, you don't," said Daff. "I don't think any sibling would even need Quint Sense to know that you absolutely have to go to the shelter tomorrow to walk Nugget the Smiling Dog."

Apple said, "Cookie, you would have to pretend for the third day in a row. That's not too much to ask?"

Cookie answered staunchly, "I will do whatever it takes to get you to walk that adorable fuzzball."

Banana rustled around. "I can pretend to be you, Apple, no problem. Everyone knows we're equally smart."

Apple said, "You mean you finally understand what I've been saying? Bicycle, can we print a map to the shelter first thing in the morning and study it? And print a backup map? And a map of where I'll walk Nugget? And a backup of that? What do we do if something breaks on my bike? Or if it rains? Do bikes function in the rain, or do they rust and stop working like the Tin Man in the Land of Oz?"

Bicycle answered, "Yes, we can bring maps and backups; I know a lot about fixing bikes, so I will come with you; we can bring raincoats; and rain doesn't hurt bikes as long as we dry them off when we get home."

Apple didn't reply for a moment. Then she said, in a

tone of awe, "I am going to walk Nugget the Smiling Dog tomorrow."

Armed with their four maps, raincoats tied around their waists despite the sunshine, Apple and Bicycle made it to the animal shelter without any wrong turns. When they parked the Fortunes, Bicycle noticed that the compass on the 713-A had begun to spin in a lazy circle.

"Is Apple's bike waking up?" she asked the Fortune as Apple walked into the shelter.

It is.

"Can you make sure it doesn't do anything to mess up Apple's dog walking?" she asked. She'd forgotten to ask it to warn her about any unusual characteristics of the 713-A.

It is an excellent bike, the Fortune reassured her.

Inside, Apple checked in at the front desk and said she'd come to volunteer as a junior dog walker. Someone had Apple fill out a form, then took her through a door where Bicycle could hear a fair amount of *woof*ing. She felt something pat her leg and looked down. A tuxedo cat, black with a white bib and two white paws, looked up at her.

"Don't mind that cat. It's haunted," the man at the shelter desk told her.

"How can a cat be haunted?" Bicycle asked.

"We've tried putting it in a cage so it can get adopted, but it somehow gets out and leaves the building. Then it comes back when it pleases. We can't figure out how it finds its way out, or in, or out again. Plus, it's been here since before I started working and never seems to age. Its eyes are, like, centuries deep, haunted by some unspeakable past."

The cat pawed Bicycle again. She considered its yellow eyes and had to admit that it had an ancient sphinx-ish look, like it knew the most disturbing secrets of the pyramids and beyond.

Apple soon came out holding a leash attached to a grinning white fuzzball. Bicycle wasn't sure which one of them was smiling more.

"Have fun with Nugget!" the shelter worker said.

"Oh, I will," Apple replied. Bicycle gave the haunted cat a little wave as they left.

As soon as they were back outside, the Fortune beeped to get Bicycle's attention. Can we please come with you? There were two teenagers checking us out and discussing whether it counted as stealing if they borrowed a bike for a ride but returned it later. I am prepared to defend the 713-A and myself if they come back, but I do not wish to make an unnecessary scene.

Bicycle relayed the Fortune's request to Apple.

"That should be okay," Apple replied. "I can hold on to the leash and the handlebars at the same time." They started to walk, and Apple commented, "Hey, the compass on my bike is working. That must be due north." She pointed the same way as the arrow was pointing, smack into the afternoon sun. "Wait, that's west."

The Fortune told Bicycle, That is not a magnetic compass. It is a more delicate and complex tool that points you toward the closest person who will change your life for the better.

She explained this to Apple, who said, "It's hard to believe my life could get better right now, but wow. Let's go that way."

Bicycle was wary, but she couldn't see how changing course could derail dog walking. They followed the not-compass's directions, which led them to a dead end facing a river. The arrow pointed into the water.

"Your bike is definitely related to my bike," said Bicycle, remembering the Fortune trying to get her to turn into the Potomac.

"Let's let Nugget explore here a little," Apple said.

The dog looked like a low-flying cloud on a leash, bounding through the grass and sniffing rocks. The darkest rock unfolded four legs and a tail and stretched, revealing itself to be the haunted cat. It didn't seem bothered by Nugget's sniffs, but it sat up straight-backed and stared at the girls.

"Is that the person who is going to change my life for the better? Do cats count as people?" Apple asked Bicycle's Fortune.

I know for a fact that our inventor considered cats to be people.

"Is that Nugget? From the television?" someone boomed in a deep, raspy voice.

A man they hadn't noticed dressed in camouflage fishing gear came up from the bank of the river. The haunted cat scampered away. Bicycle saw the man's ponytail and muttonchop whiskers and recognized Mr. Wolff, the owner of the scrapyard.

He asked, "Did you get to adopt that little darling?"

"He's not ours; we volunteered to take him on a walk," Apple told him.

Bicycle felt nervous that Mr. Wolff might recognize her or the Fortune 713-A, but he only had eyes for Nugget.

"You mean he's still available? I thought for sure I didn't have a chance, so I didn't even ask!" Mr. Wolff looked like he'd won the lottery. "Let's take him back to the shelter right now and tell them I'm ready to adopt him. I knew the minute I saw him on TV that he's the perfect dog for me." He leaned over and patted the tops of his thighs. "C'mere, Nugget!"

Nugget bounded over to him, stretching the leash to its utmost.

"Oh boy, oh boy, oh boy," Mr. Wolff rasped, scooping him up and kissing the dog's furry little head. Mr. Wolff strode back the way the girls had come.

Apple didn't have any choice but to follow, since she was still holding the other end of the leash. Passersby may have thought that the girls were taking Mr. Wolff for a walk.

When they got back to the shelter, Apple graciously gave him the leash and said, "I know you'll be happy with Nugget. He doesn't pull at his collar or bark at cats or anything like that."

Mr. Wolff thanked her and went inside.

Bicycle was impressed at her sister's noble act. "Do you want to go ask if you can walk a different dog?" Bicycle checked the clock on the Fortune's display. They'd walked Nugget for less than ten minutes. "We still have time."

"I don't know if I could handle meeting another dog yet." Apple tapped the non-compass and asked the 713-A, "Why did you send us that way? That did the opposite of improving my life."

The bike sent out a short spool of ticker tape from its handlebar stem. Apple pulled it off and showed it to Bicycle. It said: Now, the dog's life is better. Ora la vita del cane è migliore. (Italian)

Bicycle showed it to the Fortune.

The 713-A was also programmed to help its rider learn foreign languages.

Bicycle shared this with Apple, and Apple perked up a little. "How do I say 'dog' in Spanish?" The ticker tape spooled. "Japanese? Thai?" The tape continued. "Can you show it to me in all the languages you know?" The tape sped up and covered the bike frame in droopy loops. Apple couldn't keep up with reading it.

There are more than 7,000 languages spoken around the world today. The 713-A also knows dead languages like Old Norse and Latin, the Fortune blinked.

"You can stop the list, please," Apple said. The ticker tape stopped. "I understand. You pointed the way for Nugget's life to improve. Can you point for me now?"

The compass pointed back toward the dead-end street. Turning the corner was the haunted cat. It saw the girls and their bikes, and stiffened. Then it approached with its ears back, crouching low to the ground, a predator on the hunt. A few feet away, the cat lowered its head and waggled its bottom in the air, then pounced on the droopy loop of ticker tape. It batted it with one paw and twirled into the air, getting itself tangled up. It tried to free itself by twirling again, making the tangle worse. It lay on the ground and kicked the tape with its feet, *mrowl*ing as if surprised the ticker tape was winning.

"Let me give you a hand," Apple said, bending down slowly. The cat gave her its thousand-yard stare but allowed her to unravel the paper. When it was free, it crouched and bottom-waggled again. This time it leapt onto the rear rack of the 713-A. It headbutted the bike seat and blinked at Apple.

"Do you want to go for a ride?" Apple asked it. "Do cats like riding on bikes?" she asked Bicycle, who did not know either way.

Why not try? Pochemu by ne poprobovat? (Russian), a new ticker tape said.

"I guess," Apple said.

Apple and Bicycle mounted up, and the haunted cat rubbed itself against Apple's lower back and purred. It was clearly interested in a ride.

Apple told it, "If I do anything you don't like, it's not on purpose. I'm new at this."

They went to a park where they'd originally intended to walk Nugget. Apple rode with great care along a paved loop, avoiding sharp turns and bumps. The cat demonstrated a tremendous sense of balance, watching the world roll by. At the end of the park loop, it headbutted Apple fondly and leapt off the rack to the ground. It padded over to a taco cart and disappeared behind it. When Bicycle peered around the cart's side, there was no sign of the cat anywhere.

The taco vendor was closing up for the day and offered the girls his last two tacos, on the house. They crunched into the warm shells.

Bicycle wondered, *Was it the bike ride around the park or the free taco that improved Apple's life? And was it improved enough to make up for losing a walk with Nugget?*

"I wish I hadn't rushed into this," said Apple through a mouthful of cheese, meat, and taco shell. She swallowed. "If we'd had more time, I think I could have planned an adventure where everything went the way I wanted it to."

Sometimes you choose your own adventure, **the Fortune pointed out**. More often than not, though, your adventure chooses you.

Bicycle thought about that. She'd tried to combine helping her sisters with helping the 713-A, the 713-B, and the 713-D, but by doing that, three of her sisters hadn't gotten the experience they'd dreamed of. She resolved that somehow, some way, she'd make this up to Daff, Banana, and Apple—and make sure that Cookie got to eat to her heart's content.

THE VACUUM

"I'm not going," Cookie said. "I don't need to."

It had been four days since Apple had come back and told her sisters about dog walking and cat biking. The sisters had agreed that they'd do whatever it took to support Cookie having a problem-free trip to the farmers' market the next day, Saturday. But Cookie had dug in her heels and refused to even talk about it.

The girls had finally cornered her during cycling practice. "It's not fair if you don't get to go," Banana told Cookie.

Cookie answered, "I don't need it to be fair. Our plan isn't working. We were supposed to be filled with extra happiness because we'd gotten to go on adventures. Then, when Mom and Dad noticed us bubbling with yay, we were going to tell them the truth. Instead, they've noticed we're extra tired and frazzled and—what was that word Mom used? Despicable?"

"Despondent," said Apple.

It was true. Mom and Dad had wanted to check every girl's temperature after Apple's outing, because everyone was flushed—Bicycle and Apple from exercising outside on a chilly day, and Banana, Daff, and Cookie from their be-five-people efforts. Meals for this week had been quiet affairs, with no one finishing each other's sentences. Yesterday, Mom had insisted their daughters take a break from the week's chore of washing the cafeteria floor and get some extra rest because they'd been acting "despondent," one of her crossword puzzle clue words. It turned out to mean "mopey."

"I can't help moping, I didn't get to do any real karate," groused Banana.

"Every time I pick up my camera, I think that the next time I see another horror movie in a theater, I'll be a grown-up, probably devoid of creative sparks," Daff said.

"And I keep brooding over the walk I didn't get to take with Nugget," admitted Apple. "I thought I was doing a better job of hiding my feelings from Mom and Dad, but Mom keeps giving me hugs 'just because.'"

"And Mom's started sleeping on our rug again. I'm not going," said Cookie. "Let's have things go back to normal."

Banana said, "But, Cookie, you could have the perfect adventure. Then, when you come back bubbling with happiness about how you won the eating competition, your happiness will be ours, too, because we helped you do it. Mom and Dad will see it, and we'll tell them how we are ready for more independence, and then I can try again to do a karate class by myself!"

"You're our last chance," Daff said. "If this were a movie, the audience would be on the edge of their seats watching you ride toward your triumph, rooting for you, and for us."

Apple said, "We learned a lot on our three rides, and we came up with a good plan for you."

Banana waggled her eyebrows at Cookie. "It's prize-winning apple pie." Their parents had taken them to the convenience store for treats, and they'd all seen the notice about the final eating contest of the season. The bakers who'd won the top three spots at the county fair for their apple pies were providing the victuals for the contest. "And you get to bring home whatever you don't finish."

Cookie's face got dreamy. She murmured, "Pie." Then she asked Bicycle, "Do you think it's a good idea? You've gotten to see the other adventures."

Bicycle had been trying to stay out of it. She didn't want to make Cookie do anything she didn't want to. Then again, she could see how much Cookie truly did want to do this, as long as it didn't stress out her sisters and parents. It hit Bicycle that Cookie was trying to be unselfish, but at the same time was denying her true self. Bicycle knew what that felt like.

"I think it could be great," she said. "I had the Fortune ask the 713-A, 713-B, and 713-D if your bike has any unusual talents we need to be on the lookout for. Its main ability is its capacity to carry fifty times its weight in cargo. That's why your frame is thicker than anyone else's—it's super-strong, with interior chambers. The 713-C isn't going to blast music or give you strange advice or point you in the wrong direction." She added, "I'll stick with you the whole time. We can do this."

Cookie appeared on the verge of giving in. "Will you share the pie I bring home?" she asked the sisters.

"No!" Banana said. "Because you're not bringing any home. You're going to eat everything they give you and bring home a trophy, and we will be so proud of our food-devouring Cookie Monster sister. Now, will you listen to the plan we came up with?"

Cookie was ready to listen.

The next day, as she strapped on her helmet, Cookie asked her sisters, "You promise that if this goes well, we'll tell Mom and Dad tomorrow, so I don't have to keep secrets anymore?"

"Cross my heart and hope to pie," said Banana. "Ha!"

"And you also promise that if this goes wrong, we are never telling them anything and giving up on adventures?" Cookie went on.

Apple looked around at everyone, presumably reading minds. "We promise," she said. "But don't think about that now. Focus on apples and cinnamon and crust."

"Apples and cinnamon and crust," repeated Cookie. The mantra seemed to give her strength. She nodded at Bicycle, and they headed out.

Luckily, the route to the farmers' market took the girls partially on a mountain bike trail, so they didn't have much traffic to worry about. It took them longer than expected, though, because the trail was rocky and the 713-C jounced around a lot. Cookie kept wanting to stop and check whether her bike was okay. It was fine—Bicycle told Cookie it was built like a tank, and it'd take more than a rock to injure it—but Cookie wanted to make sure. By the time they got to the market, set up under an array of three-sided tents, they were late. The other eating contestants were already seated in one tent at a long table with a red-checked tablecloth, giant napkins tucked into their shirt collars.

A woman dressed in an apron stood behind a podium. She tapped on a microphone. "Is this working? Okay, we've got one seat left for the pie-eating contest. Anyone want to join in? We're going to start in a couple of minutes. First prize is fifty dollars."

"Us!" yelled Bicycle, waving. "Well, her!" She pointed at Cookie, who smiled and waved, too.

"Look at you. Come on over, honey!" the apron woman said, gesturing. "You can sit at spot number seven." She pointed Cookie over to a folding chair in front of a place setting with a big napkin, several utensils, and a glass of water.

Cookie and Bicycle parked their bikes between the tent flap and a bench covered in pie boxes. Five boxes were stacked behind a placard bearing the number seven. Cookie sat at the table and started jiggling her legs up and down.

"Settled in, honey?" the apron woman asked her.

Cookie nodded.

"Boys, could you consider letting this sweet young lady win? She's too adorable for words."

"Not for a fifty-dollar prize, I won't!" yelled out one of the "boys."

Bicycle looked at the other contestants and realized every other one of them was an adult man, most of whom were tall, solid people whose stomachs appeared to have plenty of room for food. Cookie looked like a cub among bears in comparison.

"All right, all right, but she may beat you fair and square, Takeru. Everyone, open up one of the boxes next to your number and get your first pie ready." All the contestants did so, lifting out aluminum tins filled with gorgeous full-size pies. Cookie put hers in front of her and took a big sniff. Her legs stopped jiggling.

"Let's review the rules. You can eat that pie however you see fit—utensils, hands, face—everything's fair game. You have to finish the pie down to the tin, no more than a teaspoon's worth left over. I baked some of them, so you better not waste my good cooking. You call out 'Next,' and one of the volunteers will put a fresh pie in front of you. You there"—she was addressing Bicycle—"can you help fetch your twin sister her pies?"

Bicycle nodded.

"We've got twenty minutes, and whoever eats the most pies in that time wins the prize. If it's close, we've got a scale to weigh the leftovers. Anthony was our pie champ last year"—a man who looked like a lumberjack acknowledged the crowd—"but Takeru here won this year's kielbasa-eating, ice-cream-eating, and jalapeño-eating contests, so it should be an interesting competition. Eaters ready? Yell out a 'yum' if you are!"

"Yum!" yelled the men and Cookie, sounding like they meant it.

"On your marks . . . get set . . . eat!" The apron lady started the timer.

No one used the utensils. Cookie dug both hands into her pie. Bicycle remembered how her sister had said she didn't want anyone judging her manners when she did this. Bicycle turned away to look at a display of butternut squash. The *scoop-smack-munch* sounds Cookie was making told her that her sister wasn't holding back.

Bicycle heard some of the men calling out "Next!" and was impressed when Cookie said the same only a few moments later. Bicycle opened up a new box and used the fresh apple pie to push the empty tin out of the way.

"This is so good, you should try some of it," Cookie told her. She then launched herself into the fresh one with undiminished gusto. Bicycle turned back to the butternut squash. Her sister's enthusiasm reminded her of being around some friends she'd met during the summer who ran a fried pie shop. The owner had believed that eating nothing but pie would help you live longer.

"Look at that girl go!" someone in the front row said.

"Look at Takeru, though," someone else replied.

Bicycle did. The man did not stop to chew. He gulped mouthfuls that she could almost see going down his throat in lumps. He was a human python. It was hard to watch, but hard to look away. He was well into his third pie before Cookie said, "Next!"

Bicycle tugged open the next box, but found an empty pie tin. Not totally empty—it had a few clumps of apple and flakes of crust, so it had contained a pie at some point. There was no time to wonder where it had gone, though, with Takeru pulling ahead. Bicycle put the tin on the table and opened the next box. Thankfully, this one had a full pie, which she got in front of Cookie's hands and mouth.

Bicycle tried to get the apron lady's attention about Cookie's missing pie, but a piece of the tent flap had come loose and the lady was helping some other folks set it to rights. Bicycle decided to open the fifth pie box to check what was inside, and noticed as she picked it up that a slim gray hose was attached to a hole in the side. She followed the hose with her eyes to see where it was coming from. "Oh, no," she said.

The hose was coming from the 713-C. Bicycle opened the box to see the last fragments of apple pie being vacuumed into the hose. The hose disengaged like an elephant's trunk coming out of a bag of peanuts. The 713-C withdrew the hose into its frame with a gentle *voop*.

She stood there not knowing what to do—how did you get pie out of a bicycle?—until the apron lady rang a hand-held bell and shouted, "Hands up, eaters, that's time!"

Cookie sat back and put her goop-covered hands in the air. She stretched her chin to one side and then the other and said, "Ow. I kept telling my mouth to chew faster, but my jaw got worn out. I feel like I could have eaten more if I'd had more time."

The apron lady called out, "Who's got the most empty tins? Takeru's got four, can anyone beat that?"

"The girl!" someone pointed out. "She's got three and a half empties, and her sister's holding a fourth!"

Cookie looked in confusion at Bicycle. "When I said you should try some, I didn't mean right now," she said. When the apron lady came over to check the empties, Cookie told her, "No, I ate only two and a half, so I didn't win. It was delicious trying, though." She licked some filling off her fingers. "Mmm."

The audience gave Cookie a round of applause for being

honest, and gave Takeru more applause when he collected his fifty-dollar prize. All the contestants were given extra napkins and wet wipes to clean themselves up.

"At least I get to bring this half home for later," Cookie said, picking up the tin in front of her. Bicycle heard the *voop* noise again and stared as the hose snaked out of the 713-C. It dived into Cookie's tin and vacuumed the pie away as the two sisters watched in disbelief.

"Why did my bike eat my leftovers?" Cookie asked. She asked the 713-C, "Did you take the other missing pies?"

The 713-C answered in a sweet, high-pitched voice, *"Yeff"*—how the word "yes" sounds when someone has their mouth full.

"Why?" Cookie repeated.

Bicycle could see that her easygoing sister was on the verge of losing her cool.

The gray hose extended out and touched Cookie ever so tenderly on the forearm. *"Helping."*

"But when it comes to eating, I don't need help," Cookie told it.

Bicycle said to the Fortune, "You should have stopped it. Weren't you keeping a lookout for anything unusual with the 713-C?"

The Fortune blinked, I apologize. Watching the humans eat mass quantities diverted my attention. Cookie performed admirably. Based on her pace, she could have finished five pies in thirty minutes. She should next enter an eating contest that gives her more time and more food. An hour and ten pies, perhaps.

Cookie read the Fortune's screen. "Me and ten pies to myself. That will never happen." It looked like the empty tin in her hands suddenly weighed more than she could carry. She dropped it to the table. "Let's just go home."

STAY CLOSE

Back at Twintopia, Banana saw Cookie and said, "I knew it! She hasn't got any pie with her—she won the contest!"

"Your Quint Sense is on the fritz. I didn't win, and I have no leftovers," Cookie said. "It turns out my bike eats things."

"No way," said Daff, eyeing the 713-C. "You got Shark Bike?"

The 713-C piped, *"Not eat. Save for later."* It *vooped* its hose into one of Cookie's pockets.

"Hey!" Cookie said, reaching in after it and pulling out a Skittles packet and a raisin box, both empty.

Bicycle asked the Fortune, "Did Dr. Alvarado program it this way on purpose?"

Part of the 713-C's programming is to give its rider nice surprises. It will not reveal more, but it believes with all of its circuits that it is doing a good job.

Mom and Dad came out of the apartment, Dad rubbing his hands. "Park those bikes and shake a leg, kiddos. The Gowumpkis are one of the families cooking tonight, and you know how good their kielbasa and pierogis are."

The girls' conversation was put on hold.

When Cookie didn't finish even one serving of the Polish sausage and dumplings, Mom took her temperature and sent her to bed early. Dad began noodling softly on the piano. "Who wants to learn the left-hand part to 'When the Moon Comes Over the Mountain'?"

Mom joined him on the piano bench. The other sisters pled tiredness and assembled in their room to whisper about what to do next.

"Now we give up and never tell like you promised," said Cookie. "Aaargh, not telling means keeping secrets. I hate keeping secrets."

Daff said, "Maybe we tell Mom and Dad now and emphasize what went right: how we went places and did stuff and came back safely."

"No," said Banana. "Let's all try again to see if we can actually have the experiences we planned in the first place. After we succeed, then we can tell them."

Apple said glumly, "I think we should give up. The only thing I've learned for sure is that when we start pedaling, there's no telling what might happen to us, especially with bikes like ours."

The discussion went on. Bicycle's stomach hurt the way she imagined Takeru the eating contest winner's did. She felt like she couldn't trust her instincts on how to be a good member of the Kosroy family. She was responsible for bringing the Wheels of Fortune into their lives. Life had never been too predictable with her own Fortune, but she'd gone along with the idea of trying bicycle adventures even when she knew they'd be full of surprises. She imagined her parents' faces when they found out that her return had stirred up this sneaky behavior. She should have talked her sisters out of pedaling into the unknown.

Apple asked, "What do you think, Bicycle?"

Bicycle faked a yawn and a too-sleepy-to-figure-it-out mumble. She could feel Apple gazing at her, but her sister just said, "Okay," and didn't press for more.

In the morning, Dad was up before Mom, brewing a batch of some new hyperstrong coffee he'd ordered through the mail. He poured two travel mugs full of the smoky-smelling liquid and told the girls he was bringing them over to the Lakshmis' place. "Kulsoom and Rahi said they're so tired, they need to drink coffee first to figure out how to make more coffee."

The sisters shuffled around, getting dressed. The mood was low. Bicycle lectured herself that starting today, she'd be a better daughter who followed the rules, stayed close, and convinced her sisters to do the same. Her instincts would henceforth be ignored. Riding in the hallway would be enough.

There was a sound of voices and a bit of commotion in the hallway. Dad came in, frowning deeply. When Bicycle saw that he was holding four one-hundred-thousand-dollar bills, she froze.

"Wow, Dad, is that real money? Are we rich now?" Banana asked. She didn't wait for an answer and came to pluck one of the bills from his hand.

"Someone just told me that you gave it to them," he said, befuddled. "Well, he said Belladonna Kosroy gave it to him, which I assume is you, even though that makes no sense."

"No sense," Banana agreed. "Like I'd give these away. If I had some hundred-thousand-dollar bills, I'd use them to buy an airplane. No, a private island. No, a talking walrus. Can I choose all of the above?"

Apple asked, "Hundred-thousand-dollar bills?" She took another one from Dad and examined it. "These can't be real. I think the government only printed them after the Great Depression for banks to transfer money to other banks."

Dad said, "They're not real. That's what this guy in the hallway just told me. He said someone named Belladonna Kosroy used this money to buy those bikes we found in the property room, but when he tried to use the four hundred thousand dollars to purchase a building, the real estate agent told him it was counterfeit."

"Counterfeit?" said Apple, turning to Bicycle.

"Our bikes?" said Cookie, turning to Bicycle.

"Four hundred thousand dollars?" said Daff, turning to Bicycle.

"Oh, Belladonna Kosroy, right!" said Banana. "Oh. Oh! Ohhhh." She turned to Bicycle. "I mean, we have no idea what that guy was talking about." She gave her sisters a volcanically intense glare, so the other three turned away from Bicycle and looked anywhere but at her. Bicycle stayed still, hoping the floor would swallow her up.

The Fortune blinked, Next time I will print four hundred $1,000 bills instead, or four thousand $100 bills, which would weigh 8 pounds and 13 ounces and require a sturdy bag in which to carry them.

"He had a receipt," Dad went on, holding up a flimsy yellow piece of paper. "This says Chuck Wolff sold four bikes to Belladonna Kosroy and delivered them to this address a week and a half ago. But since payment was invalid, he came to repossess the bikes."

"What does that mean, 'repossess'?" asked Cookie.

"He took the bikes away," Dad answered.

Apple, Banana, Cookie, and Daff started talking at

once. "What?" "You let him take them? Dad, no!" "They're gone?" "We have to get them back!" "I need to teach my bike not to eat stuff!" "Who will play a soundtrack to my life now?" "I can't grow up to a be a famous racer without that bike!" "Mine is teaching me Latin and Greek!"

Bicycle's heart dropped to her knees. The one thing she'd done right—saving the Fortunes—had come undone.

Mom, hunched over and droopy-eyed, emerged from the bedroom. "Loud for morning," she grumbled. She came to give Dad a good-morning kiss and noticed the money in his hands. "Did we get paid for something?" She squinted hard. "How many zeroes are on those?"

"We might be able to catch him before he leaves," Apple said. "Come on, everybody."

The girls scrambled to put on shoes. Cookie yanked open the door, and Bicycle felt her heart rise a few inches to see her sisters' innate reaction to losing their bikes was determination to get them back. Maybe the Fortunes hadn't ruined as much as she'd thought they had.

"Whoa, whoa," said Mom. "Someone needs to tell me what is happening."

Cookie shouted over her shoulder, "There's no time!" She ran out with Daff, who said, "We're going out front." Apple followed hot on their heels and added, "We'll explain after."

Bicycle put her hands on the Fortune's handlebars. Her

instincts were demanding that she launch herself out the door with the Fortune and offer Chuck eight pounds and thirteen ounces of hundred-dollar bills, but that wasn't something a decent member of society raised by Sister Wanda would do. A good, stay-close daughter definitely wouldn't do it, either. She wavered uncertainly until Banana grabbed her arm.

"No time to think, it's time to go," Banana said, her forward momentum propelling both them and the Fortune after their sisters.

The girls tore through Twintopia, but they weren't fast enough. By the time they got outside, Chuck's pickup was already pulling out of the driveway. It looked like he'd thrown the bikes willy-nilly into the bed of the truck. One sideways tire bounced up and down on top, woefully waving good-bye.

"Come back here and let's settle this like geese!" yelled Banana, shaking her fist as the truck accelerated away.

Cookie said in a hushed voice, "He's going to melt them, isn't he?"

"Yes," said Bicycle, digging her fingernails into the Fortune's handlebar tape. "So he can sell their metal for four hundred thousand real dollars, instead of the money the Fortune printed for me."

"You can print money?" Apple asked the Fortune.

It printed her a two-dollar bill.

Twintopia's double doors opened behind them. Mom and Dad stood in the doorway. They'd thrown coats over top of their pajamas. "What are you doing out there?" Dad demanded.

Banana replied, "In a nutshell, this dude took our bikes, which Bicycle bought for us with fake money because they're intelligent and almost alive, and he's going to melt them at a scrapyard."

Mom announced, "You girls have been acting strangely all week, but this takes the cake. Get back inside right now."

The Fortune blasted a piece of music that made them all jump, an aching sob begging not to be forgotten.

Daff turned to the Fortune and said, "That's the 713-D transmitting to you, isn't it?"

The bike responded, It is. The bikes do not understand what is happening to them. We cannot wait. An industrial crucible's furnace can reach 1,000 degrees Fahrenheit in less than half an hour.

Bicycle couldn't look at Mom and Dad. Breaking their rules right in front of their eyes made her heart hurt. She climbed aboard the Fortune's seat and said to her sisters, "I'll go fix this. I'll take all the blame once I get back." She hoped her parents wouldn't regret that she'd returned home and turned their lives upside down.

"I'm coming with you!" Banana said. "You'll need

someone who knows at least one karate move. Make room, I'm getting on."

"Did anyone hear me?" said Mom.

"I'm coming, too," said Apple. "I'm the smart one, after all. Can I ride on the rear rack?"

"The 713-C needs me to come, too," said Cookie.

Daff said, "Please don't leave me behind to explain this to Mom and Dad without a script."

I can take one other rider, the Fortune blinked. It vibrated and buzzed. Its frame grew longer. It sprouted an additional seat, plus an extra set of handlebars and pedals to match. It was now a two-seater tandem bike.

Bicycle thought, *It's official. I'm never going to stop being surprised by the Fortune.* A brief scuffle started among the girls over who would get the new tandem seat.

Their parents gave up on waiting for them to come inside of their own accord and stomped out of the building toward them.

Dad's annoyed voice separated the sisters' scuffle. "What are you thinking? Didn't you hear your mother? Back inside this instant!"

Apple spoke first. "We're sorry. We know this scares you, but we're not letting you stop us this time. We're going to rescue our bikes."

"This time?" Mom said. "What is that supposed to mean?"

Banana said, "Do you have any idea how much stuff we never try to do so you won't be upset? This is too important. Our bikes are going to be melted into oblivion! We're not going to pretend it's okay to protect your feelings."

Cookie leapt in to add, "We know you want us to stay home because you love us. It's just hard sometimes."

Mom's mouth opened and shut soundlessly. She looked at Dad, who looked like horrifically sticky Band-Aids were being peeled off his entire body.

The Fortune flashed its screen to get the parents' attention. I understand how out of control you feel when contemplating any member of your family being in danger, away from your protection. You wish to keep them safe in any way you can. You would hide them in a closet wrapped in bubble wrap if you could.

Mom nodded a small nod.

I feel the same about my siblings, the missing bikes. But they could not be fully aware without being allowed to move in the sunshine. I think humans are like this, too.

I know you do your best. The other Fortunes do their best to take care of Apple, Banana, Cookie, and Daff. Please help your girls return the favor now.

"Your bike really can communicate," Dad said faintly.

Bicycle squeezed the Fortune's handlebars. She truly did not know what she'd do if Dad demanded she get off the bike or if Mom started to cry.

Instead of crying, Mom took a breath that expanded her belly. She then spoke in a deep, resounding voice completely unlike her own. Bicycle thought the universe itself may have been speaking through her.

She said, "None of you are getting on this bike. I am."

DOING THE BEST YOU CAN

"Now, I put my feet on these thingies, right?" Mom said in her regular voice, awkwardly climbing onto the Fortune's extra seat and nudging at a pedal with her shin.

Bicycle wanted to ask a dozen different questions, but she didn't want to break whatever spell had transformed their mom. The rest of the family didn't seem to feel the same compunction.

"Who are you and what have you done with our mother?" Banana asked.

"You took the words right out of my mouth," Apple joined in.

Daff muttered, "I can't imagine any background music that would make sense of this."

"Do you know how to use the brakes?" asked Cookie.

Dad said, "Stella, what about your eyesight?"

Mom answered, "Bicycle can see where we're going, so my eyesight doesn't matter. I've got this." Bicycle couldn't see her mother's face when she said these last three words, but everyone else could, and whatever they saw made them take a step back.

"Right," Dad said. He repeated it again, nodding. "Right. Cookie, go to our apartment and get helmets for your mother and Bicycle."

Cookie ran in and returned in a flash.

Dad clapped Bicycle on the shoulder and told her, "Well, if you want anyone at your side in a strange situation, it's your mother. Come on, girls. The rest of you can explain what's going on, and we'll figure out what we can do on this end."

Apple, Banana, Cookie, and Daff allowed themselves to be herded back toward the building, casting mystified looks over their shoulders at the two-person Fortune.

"Mom," Bicycle said. She hoped she could impress upon her mother how important this was in the fewest possible words. "We have to go fast."

"Well, what are we waiting for?" Mom asked. "You taught your sisters how to ride, and now you can teach me. How do we start?" She pushed her right pedal, and Bicycle's own pedal crank turned in tandem. The Fortune moved a half-wheel rotation forward.

"That's how we start," said Bicycle. She suddenly realized her mother was about to have a front-row seat to Bicycle being truly herself. She hoped that Mom would like what she saw. "Hold on to the handlebars and do what I do."

Bicycle had never captained a tandem bike before, but one thing she knew was that with their extra weight, gravity had a lot of influence on their downhill speed. When they started down the first hill, she told her mom how to keep her body balanced while they coasted. She listened hard for Mom getting upset or scared. Instead, she heard her say with a sound of wonder in her voice, "So this is what it feels like." Then Mom pushed her pedals harder to speed them up even more.

Bicycle felt a smile creep onto her face.

They made it to the closed gate of the scrapyard as fast as Bicycle could have wished.

Mom got off the bike first and said with satisfaction, "Did it." She asked Bicycle, "Now we need to get in there and talk someone out of melting your bikes, correct?"

Bicycle nodded, peering inside. She saw no sign of Chuck's truck.

Mom tugged on the gate, but it didn't budge. "Maybe they're not here yet," Mom said. "Could we have gotten here faster than someone driving?"

We could have, but we did not. Look at the crumbs on the ground.

Bicycle saw a precise line of pale brown crumbs that led from the driveway into the scrapyard and down an alleyway between twin mountains of soda cans. She bent down to examine them and caught a whiff of cinnamon and apples.

"Pie-crust crumbs." She then noticed three strips of paper that said, Help! Hilfe! (German) Help! Aidez-moi! (French) Help! Greiða! (Old Norse). She said, "They're here."

Mom found an intercom box labeled PRESS HERE FOR SERVICE. She buzzed the buzzer button to get someone's attention. Nothing happened. There were no lights on in the office trailer that Bicycle could see.

A tuxedo cat with ancient eyes appeared from nowhere and began rubbing up against Mom's leg. "Hello," Mom said, and scratched behind its ears. The cat looked as though this were one more memory to add to eons of memories.

Bicycle was sure this was the haunted cat from the shelter. She petted the cat's back, and it arched up under her hand. She murmured to it, "I wish you could open gates the same way you open cages and doors."

The haunted cat blinked at Bicycle a couple of times. It lolloped away.

"Hey, hold on, how did the cat get over there? That is the same cat that was just here a second ago, isn't it?" said Mom, pointing at a tuxedo cat now strolling past them on the other side of the gate. It twitched its tail at Bicycle with a smug expression that said, *In my long life, I have learned how to open everything.* It padded over to a mechanism attached to the chain-link fence and headbutted the switch. The mechanism turned, and the gate creaked its way open.

The cat melted into the shadows and was gone.

"Well. That's the most helpful cat I've ever met." Mom took a few steps into the scrapyard and said, "Oh my. This looks like a dangerous place to wander around."

The Fortune blinked, It has been more than thirty minutes. We must hurry.

"You can wait here if you're scared," Bicycle told her mom. "The Fortune and I will figure something out."

Mom's forehead wrinkled. "I have given you a poor impression of myself, kiddo. I wasn't scared of anything before I had you and your sisters. As you grew, I had to cope with my heart walking around outside my body five times over." She jutted out her chin. "That's no excuse for putting my fears first for so long, though."

It occurred to Bicycle that maybe while she was wondering what Mom would think of her, her mother was feeling exposed, too.

Mom looked at the line of crumbs. "That way, right?"

She marched forward. Bicycle pushed the Fortune after her. A few aisles through the junk, they found the 713-B lying askew against a row of toilet bowls.

"Banana's bike!" Bicycle exclaimed. She pulled it upright and asked it, "Did you fall off the truck? Are you okay? I'm sorry I let you get taken. Where are the other bikes?"

The messages glowed. YES, INDEED. YES, INDEED. YOU ARE DOING THE BEST YOU CAN, AND SO IS EVERYONE ELSE. TURN LEFT. SEEK SHELTER.

"Seek shelter?" Mom asked it.

Then they heard the growl. Bicycle's mind leapt like a gazelle toward the memory of the scrapyard office's sign with the picture of the German shepherd: I CAN MAKE IT TO THE FENCE IN 2.8 SECONDS. CAN YOU?

Mom pushed Bicycle behind her, went up on her tiptoes, and shouted, "Go away!" in the general direction of the growling sound.

Nugget floated out from behind a toilet with a tough look on his fluffy white face. "Awww!" Bicycle said.

Nugget immediately gave her a doggy smile. *Was my growling good?* his expression said. *I am good at things!* He was trailing a length of twine behind him. It looked like he'd been tied up but gotten loose.

Mom said, "Watch out. I've had some painful lessons about trusting dogs."

She made sure Bicycle stayed behind her, knotted her hands into fists, and approached the puppy as if it were a ticking bomb. Nugget's pink tongue lolled out as Mom edged cautiously nearer. Anyone else might have thought her silly for approaching this little cloud of a dog like he might detonate, but Bicycle saw the situation for what it was: her mother being brave. Mom bent over in slow motion and wrapped the twine around her wrist. Nugget wagged his tail with joy.

"Okay, I've got him."

Bicycle heard an insanely loud blast of the song "You're

a Mean One, Mr. Grinch" from up ahead, followed by an "OW!" and a string of curse words. Bicycle said in a whisper, "I bet that's Chuck. Maybe the Fortunes are fighting back."

We are programmed to persist, the Fortune blinked.

"Well, now they've got us to fight for them," Mom said.

She pushed the 713-B toward the sounds, Nugget at her heels. Bicycle and the Fortune followed closely. They came upon Chuck two alleys away, standing next to a shiny, cylindrical machine with a conveyer belt that Bicycle assumed was the crucible. Chuck had his cowboy hat in his hands and was wiping something off the brim. Bicycle could see his jaw muscles clenched around the thick toothpick in his mouth. This one said FREE. His truck was parked to the side with the tailgate door open. The 713-A, 713-C, and 713-D lay tangled together inside.

The 713-D noticed them before Chuck did. It erupted into a cacophony of classical music. *HALLELUJAH!* sang a chorus. *HALLELUJAH! HAL-LEY-LU-YAH!* From the bed of the truck, the 713-C *voop*ed out its hose and shot a glob of pie that hit Chuck in the belly.

He crammed his hat back on his head and said, "Stop doing that!"

The 713-C responded by shooting a barrage of globs that covered him from shoulders to feet.

"Yes!" Bicycle couldn't help but cheer for the 713-C.

Chuck turned toward her and narrowed his eyes. "Ms. Kosroy's assistant, what are you doing here?" He sized up Mom. "And you," he said, "must be Ms. Kosroy." He noticed Nugget, smiling in every direction. "Shoot. I was trying to turn that puppy into a watchdog."

"He seems too sweet for that," Mom said, offering Chuck the twine leash, which he snatched out of her hand.

Chuck rolled his toothpick from one corner of his mouth to the other and growled at Mom, "You can't treat people like you treat pigs. You're not welcome on this property." He lifted Nugget into the pickup truck's cab and shut the door.

Mom appeared briefly taken aback, but she recovered by smoothing her pajama pants and clearing her throat. "I am Stella Kosroy, and I'm not sure why you're talking about pigs. There was a misunderstanding this morning. We need these bikes back. My daughters love them. Can we come to some sort of agreement?"

"Heck, no!" Chuck said. "You Kosroy people gave me funny money. I don't trust you."

"Funny money?" Mom said, baffled.

Bicycle said to Chuck, "The counterfeit money was a mistake, but we can pay you real money this time. Just not as much."

Mom gave Bicycle a keen look that clearly meant, *You will explain the counterfeit money later.* She then turned to

231

Chuck and said, "I assure you, there will be *no* counterfeit money going forward." She pulled her wallet out of her coat pocket and said, "I have forty-eight dollars for a down payment now, and I'm happy to arrange a payment plan." She laid the money on the end of the tailgate.

"Are you kidding me? Forty-eight dollars isn't going to let me open my own business," Chuck said. He took the bills, though.

Bicycle figured that he'd now gotten three dollars more than she owed him, so they were square.

Chuck grabbed the 713-A from the truck and pulled it to the ground. The not-compass spun in an agitated circle and started spewing ticker tape. Chuck scooped up a piece, read it, and scowled.

"What does it say?" Bicycle asked.

"That my grandmother would be ashamed of me. Then it says it in Pig Latin." He said to the bike, "No, she wouldn't! She'd understand. She knew I never belonged in scrap work." He pulled the 713-D down and asked it, "Would you shut up?" It changed its music from the "Hallelujah Chorus" back to "You're a Mean One, Mr. Grinch."

A chirpy whistle pierced the air, and a nearby voice rasped, "Nugget, here, boy! Where's my sweet Nuggety-Nug-Nug?"

Bicycle could see Nugget start to boing up and down inside the cab of the pickup truck. The haunted cat sauntered into the alleyway. Hot on its heels followed Mr. Wolff, who whistled again for Nugget. The cat leapt gracefully onto the truck's hood and from there to the roof of the cab, where it proceeded to lick a paw and clean its ears.

"There's my boy!" said Mr. Wolff, pulling open the truck's door and catching Nugget, who sprang into his arms. "And there's my other boy," he said in a frustrated tone, looking at Chuck. "You put this rope on him? I told you, I don't want to train him to be a guard dog. I want him to be a greeter dog, an animal who welcomes people. I swear, sometimes I feel like the things I say to you go in one ear and out the other."

Chuck just clamped his mouth around his toothpick and tugged the 713-C out of the pickup bed.

Mr. Wolff noticed Bicycle and her mother. "Oh, hello. Are you the Kosroy folks who called a few minutes ago about the bikes? I think I talked to someone named Alex."

"That is my husband," said Mom. "Yes, we're here to get those bikes back, please." She gestured at the Fortunes at Chuck's feet.

"Well, we made a deal over the phone, and they're all yours. Working bikes need riders, not recycling. C'mon, Chuck, let's get this sorted out."

Chuck shook his head violently. "Dad, you're making a mistake. These bikes are worth a lot of money."

At his feet, the 713-A's not-compass needle spun even faster.

Mr. Wolff answered, "You know my philosophy—treating people well is more important than chasing after profits. We act right, and enough money will follow. Did that go in one ear and out the other, too?"

"Aargh!" Chuck burst out. "What about me telling you I'd found the perfect location to start my custom-carved toothpick business, and I need the down payment for the building now? Did that go in any of your ears?"

Mr. Wolff said patiently, "We've been over this. Starting a business is risky, son. You're better off here with me. There's always job security in scrap."

Chuck muttered, "I don't want security. I want to do what I'm good at." He looked defeated, like he knew arguing wouldn't make any difference.

The 713-A's needle stopped revolving and pointed straight and true at Bicycle. She tried to think of the best thing she could do to help right now. She was suddenly gripped by the overpowering feeling that she should move to the side, and that she should make her mother do the same. It was almost as if four voices within her skull were shouting, *Get out of the way!*

Mom gave both Mr. Wolff and Chuck a sympathetic look. "Sometimes we think we're doing the right thing by protecting our kids, but sometimes we need to—" She let out a very surprised *yip* as Bicycle grabbed her arm and yanked her sideways, away from Chuck.

The alleyway filled with Kosroy girls, led by Banana windmilling her arms and yelling, "It's time to REAP THE WHIRLWIND!"

She was followed closely by Apple, Cookie, Daff, and, finally, a goose hissing like it had swallowed every rattlesnake in the world.

WE ARE *NOT* RIDING FIFTY MILES

The girls came to a skidding halt in front of the crucible. "Go get him!" Banana said to Goose Lee, pointing at Chuck.

Goose Lee barely looked at Chuck, though. Instead, he swayed his neck back and forth, focusing on Cookie with hungry menace.

"How did you get here?" Mom asked the girls.

No one answered her. All eyes were on the goose. Mr. Wolff hugged Nugget protectively. The haunted cat stopped washing its ears and looked intrigued.

"I don't have any more raisins," Cookie pleaded with Goose Lee. She pulled two pockets inside out to show it. Goose Lee advanced another step, clearly unconvinced that Cookie's other pockets might not hold more tasty treasure.

"Don't get *her*, get *him*!" Banana said, now pointing with both hands. "Isn't it obvious who's a good guy or a bad guy?"

"What are you doing?" Bicycle asked her.

236

Banana, trying to redirect the single-minded Goose Lee, said tensely, "We used raisins to lead Goose Lee here to scare Chuck into giving us our bikes back. Isn't it obvious?"

Chuck said, "You thought I'd be scared of a goose?"

Goose Lee gave Chuck a squinty glare.

Chuck took a step back and said, "Is it just me, or does that thing look kind of like Clint Eastwood?"

The 713-D played a strain of music from the final stand-off duel in the Clint Eastwood movie *The Good, the Bad, and the Ugly*. Daff looked inspired. She stepped forward, holding her fist in front of her, and yelled, "I'm the one with the raisins. Can't you tell us apart?" The goose whipped his head around and waddled her way.

Apple waved both her arms. "No, you dumb goose, I'm the one with the raisins!"

Goose Lee changed direction and headed for Apple.

Bicycle caught on to the goose-distraction game and jumped up and down. "No, it's me!"

Mom stepped in, too. "Don't you mess with my daughters," she told the goose.

Dad came running in from the same direction as the sisters, panting. "Don't you mess with my family!"

Goose Lee raised his wings and spun in a circle, honking furiously at each of them, announcing that if he needed to obliterate the entire Kosroy family plus the entire planet to get what he wanted, so be it.

No one backed down. Bicycle felt proud that these were her people.

The 713-C piped up with its my-mouth-is-full voice. *"I haf de raisins!"* Then it blew a bunch of nature's candy onto Chuck. The dried fruits stuck like flies to the pie globs already studding his clothes.

Goose Lee's beady eyes widened. There was no missing now that this was the person who had the raisins.

Chuck never stood a chance. The goose flapped up into the air and dive-bombed him. Chuck yelped and covered his head, which Goose Lee interpreted as an attempt to hog all the yummies stuck to the hat. Chuck turned and ran from the resulting whirlwind of screeching feathers. Goose Lee gave chase.

"Son!" yelled Mr. Wolff. Nugget barked valiantly and leapt to the ground. The two of them sprinted after Chuck and the goose. The haunted cat leapt down from the truck's roof and padded behind them, tail high, looking like it hadn't had this much excitement in millennia.

The girls immediately grabbed their bikes. Cookie told the 713-C, "You are a good bike, yes, you are! You're my Fortune and I'm your Cookie, so together we're a Fortune Cookie!"

Banana took the 713-B from Mom and said, "See, I knew our plan would work perfectly."

"This was a plan?" asked Mom, frowning at the sounds of honking and yelling reverberating from the far side of the scrapyard. "Maybe we should go after them. I know geese don't actually have teeth, but still."

"I think Goose Lee will calm down once he eats," Banana said.

Apple added, "But just in case that goose now has the impression that we are the source of the world's raisins, we should probably get out of here."

"I second that," Dad said. "Can any of these other bikes grow an extra seat for me?"

Daff's 713-D agreeably expanded the same way the Fortune had into a two-seater bike.

Dad said, "Just let me drop off the money for the bikes at the office before we leave."

Bicycle told him Mom had already given Chuck forty-eight dollars, but Mom waved that information away and said, "Let that poor man save it towards his toothpick business." Dad jogged over to the office trailer and back.

Just outside the entrance to the scrapyard, one of the free shuttle buses was waiting. The driver called to Dad, "Praise be, you're okay! After I saw that creature chasing the girls, I didn't know if I should call the police or what."

As he spoke, Bicycle noticed a goose-shaped shadow arise from the scrapyard and flap its way west. Goose Lee appeared to be heading home. The shadow let out a victorious honk that filled the sky, and Bicycle knew that Chuck was no longer covered in raisins.

"No, we're fine, we got the bikes and the, er, creature is gone," Dad said. "Thanks again for giving us a ride."

The driver waved both hands in an aw-shucks motion. "I had to help you. Can't stand when someone cries, let alone four someones. Don't forget to grab those helmets you left on the front seat." Apple climbed the bus steps to gather them. "Stay safe. See you 'round." He rolled up his window and drove away.

"You were smart to suggest that we turn on some tears," Apple said to Daff.

Mom waved a hand above her head as if flagging down a taxi. She said, "I would like to say that I am very confused by many things that have happened this morning. Help me out."

Dad told Mom, "I'll tell you what happened after you left Twintopia: your girls were brilliant. First, they had me call the scrapyard and, when no one answered, everyone with the last name of Wolff in the phone book until we found the scrapyard owner. They told me to offer to bring him their saved allowance money to buy the bikes back. He said that would be plenty and we could meet him in the scrapyard. Then they ran down to see if we could switch days to borrow the commune's car. When we realized the car was already gone, we went to talk to the shuttle bus drivers."

Apple said, "That was your idea, Dad."

Daff said, "But I came up with pretending to cry to

convince someone to give us a ride to a location off the regular bus route."

Cookie said, "It wasn't hard to do—thinking of our bikes melting into sad little pools of metal." She sniffed and patted the 713-C. "You can eat whatever you want."

"Not eat, save for later," the bike burbled.

"Where did that demented goose come from?" Mom asked.

"I don't know." Dad squinted at Banana. "Did that have something to do with the detour you told the bus driver to take, and Cookie throwing stuff out the window?"

"Yes!" beamed Banana. "I felt certain we could convince Goose Lee into supporting our righteous cause if we left him a trail of temptation."

Mom studied Banana. She asked, "What else do I not know about my daughters' lives?"

Banana answered, "Nothing important. Let's hear more of what Dad is saying."

Dad continued, "That's kind of the end of my story. After we got here, that demon-bird came at us and we ran. Daff heard loud music playing, and we made a beeline for that. You know what happened next. So here we are."

"Yes. Here we are, in a scrapyard. Early in the morning. Atop bikes I thought were Twintopia property, that you then bought over the phone, which we had to free from captivity," Mom said. "We are going home now so that I can talk to each of my children and find out the 'unimportant' details that I'm missing."

She gave Bicycle the same look she'd given when she'd heard about the counterfeit money, and Bicycle felt her face grow hot.

"Which way is home?" Mom asked.

Bicycle pointed.

Mom squinted at the road. "Ah. So it's uphill most of the way back, then." She climbed onto the Fortune's back seat.

Bicycle answered, "Pretty much." She wondered what would happen when they got home. They'd for sure have to tell their parents about their secret cycling trips. Would Mom and Dad decide they now needed to keep their daughters under closer scrutiny? Was this moment in the chilled November air their last taste of cycling freedom? She put her right foot on a pedal, but couldn't make herself push it forward.

No one else started pedaling either. The family sort of shuffled around in the brief silence.

"I'm just going to say it," said Apple. "I don't want to go home."

Cookie agreed softly, "Me neither."

Daff said, "Me three-neither."

Banana said, "I don't want this morning to end. I mean, think about what we did. Look at us here, right now. A family on a real adventure! Once we get back to normal life, what are the odds Mom is ever getting on a bike again?"

Mom huffed.

Bicycle felt compelled to tell her sisters, "You should have seen her. She figured out how to ride in no time. And she's not afraid to go fast. In fact, she wasn't afraid of anything we faced."

Dad said, "I knew when I met her that Stella Kosroy was an unstoppable force."

Bicycle was the only one close enough to Mom to hear her murmur, "I'm still an unstoppable force." Bicycle thought about her mother pushing her pedals harder on the downhill. She thought about her striding into the unknown dangers of the scrapyard. She saw her picking up Nugget's leash even though she didn't know if Nugget was a rabid watchdog. Maybe the third rule of family belonging wasn't Be Who They Need You to Be. Maybe each member should help the others Be Who They Already Are.

Bicycle craned her face over her shoulder to catch Mom's eye. "Let's show them."

Bicycle found the emotions darting across her mom's face hard to read. What mattered most, though, was the final one that landed in place and held fast: determination.

Mom settled her glasses more firmly on her nose and placed her foot on a pedal. "Where to?"

"We could go to a karate dojo," said Banana.

"We could visit the animal shelter," suggested Apple.

"Is anyone hungry? We didn't have breakfast yet,"

mentioned Cookie. The 713-C gave her something that looked like a handful of Skittle pie.

"Too early for a movie matinee," sighed Daff.

"A cup of hot coffee would hit the spot," said Dad.

Bicycle let everyone else's comments sail past. Then she answered Mom's question with a question. "If you and I could ride this bike anywhere, where would you want to go?" She opened her heart to listen, really listen, to the answer.

Mom looked up at the sky. "Somewhere that I can have fun with my family."

Turn right, suggested the Fortune.

Bicycle wasn't sure where that would lead them. The Fortune showed her a map, and she saw a great idea. "Okay. We're turning right. Downhill, at least at first." This was her chance to show Mom and Dad that bicycling didn't have to be done only in hallways or on emergency rescue missions. She turned and felt the extra power when Mom's pedal stroke joined hers. The rest of the family fell in behind, single-file. The girls whooped encouragement to their mother. Bicycle heard the 713-D begin playing an energetic, guitar-filled song.

Dad said, "Now *this* is how I remember cycling."

Minutes later, they were on the C&O Canal Towpath, the paved trail that had led Bicycle to Harpers Ferry from Washington, D.C.

"How neat," Dad said. "Where does this trail go?"

Bicycle pointed her arms out scarecrow-style. "To the left, it leads to Maryland. To the right, it goes to D.C. and my Mostly Silent Monastery, about fifty miles from here. The trail is basically flat, and cars are not allowed on it, and there are definitely no gopher holes. We could ride two-by-two, even three-by-two, as long as we always make room for folks coming the other direction."

"Goodness, I didn't know there were bike paths that went for more than fifty miles," Mom said.

The Fortune blinked. The Mickelson Trail in South Dakota is 109 miles long. The Great Allegheny Passage through Maryland and Pennsylvania is 150 miles long. The Katy Trail in Missouri is 240 miles long. The East Coast Greenway leads 3,000 miles from the coastal tip of Maine to the islands of Key West, Florida.

Bicycle didn't share any of this. The timing wasn't right.

"We can totally ride fifty miles!" said Banana. "Let's do it as fast as we can. If we go fifty miles an hour, we'll be at Bicycle's monastery in an hour. Is that normal cycling speed?"

"No, normal speed is closer to ten miles an hour," Bicycle told her. "I didn't mean we should ride fifty miles—"

Apple interrupted, "If we can average ten miles an hour, we could be in Washington in five hours. That's not too much."

Daff said, "The movie theater is a mile and a half from home. I think I could do that twenty-five times."

"We are *not* riding fifty miles!" Mom protested. "We don't have anything to eat, we might get lost, and Dad and I are in our pajamas, for heaven's sake!"

Bicycle knew this was pushing too far, too fast. She tried to rein in her sisters' enthusiasm. "I thought we could ride a mile or two together, that's it."

"This is a great place for us to show that we're way more independent and capable now than they realize," Apple told Bicycle. She then addressed Mom. "Dad explained that your priorities changed when you had us. That means they could change again."

Banana said, "You don't need to take care of us like we're little kids anymore."

Cookie said, "We can try new things, and do some of them on our own." Her stomach let out a loud grumble.

"I help," announced the 713-C. It *voop*ed and gave each of them a tube of bread filled with something.

Cookie took a bite of hers. "This tastes like an egg-and-cheese biscuit. Where'd you get these?"

"Made them," the 713-C said.

"From what?"

"Food," it answered. *"All food is made from food."* Another slot opened in its frame, from which a tray emerged. The bike presented Mom and Dad tiny ceramic cups full of black liquid.

The Fortune told Bicycle, The 713-C means that the molecules in any food can be rearranged into any other

246

food. While it is unnecessary to make anything more than Complete Nutrition pellets, Dr. Alvarado must have programmed the 713-C to take in ingredients and transform them into any dish it chooses.

Dad sipped his cup. "Espresso. Thank you. These are really high-end bikes, aren't they?"

We take good care of our riders, the Fortune blinked. Tell your parents they don't have to keep you fed, sheltered, and safe by themselves. They have us now.

The 713-A sent out a ticker tape, and Apple read it. "My bike says wherever I go, it will help keep me pointed in the right direction. Then it says it in Polish." Bicycle noticed that the compass needle was turning to point deliberately at each family member in turn.

The 713-B's whatsis glowed, and Banana said, "My bike is telling us we never know until we try. Also, to turn right. Also, to snack." She took a bite of her biscuit tube.

The 713-D launched into a medley of happy songs. Then it picked out three words and repeated them several times: "We are family. We are family."

"My bike is singing what I would like to say," Daff told the group.

"Is bike riding usually like this?" Mom asked Bicycle.

Bicycle answered truthfully, "It's always full of surprises."

Mom pressed her hands together over her heart and cleared her throat to get everyone's attention. "I repeat, we are *not* riding fifty miles this morning. But I'll make a deal with you. We can ride a couple of miles together on this pretty path. Then we go home, and we plan how we're going to ride fifty miles on a family adventure to Bicycle's monastery. We can do that, can't we?" she asked Dad.

Dad grinned. "I think we can."

Bicycle's heart swelled. She couldn't wait to tell Sister Wanda that her family was going to cycle to the monastery to meet everyone.

"Promise?" said Banana. "I mean, no matter what we tell you about the details of our lives later, you won't change your mind?"

Mom cocked her head, considering. She said, "I promise. It sounds like you have a lot to say that you haven't been saying. Dad and I will make sure we listen to you. I've known things had to change for a while now, but I guess I needed a kickstart."

Or a nice long ride in the sunshine, thought Bicycle.

WOO

A week later, Bicycle woke up with the haunted cat on her chest.

When they'd left the bike path, the cat had come galloping up to them near the convenience store in Harpers Ferry. Apple had stopped to pet it, and it had jumped onto the rear rack of her bike to accompany them home. Throughout the week, it kept disappearing and reappearing all over Twintopia. It had met the Lakshmi family and proved itself mysteriously able to put all of the quadruplet boys to sleep at the same time by running its tail over their foreheads. Mr. and Mrs. Lakshmi showered the cat with love and tuna treats.

The cat had accompanied the family on a bike ride nearly every day. It always wanted to ride with Apple, so Apple borrowed the flowery wicker basket from the little bike in the property room and affixed it to the 713-A's handlebars as a kitty carrier. These family bike rides had taken several forms: all seven Kosroys together, just one parent and one daughter, just the sisters as a group, just two sisters together.

One night when they were in their bunk beds, Bicycle asked Apple, Banana, Cookie, and Daff if they'd felt like these family bike rides were too much togetherness.

Cookie had answered, "If whomever you're with is having genuine fun doing the same thing you're doing, togetherness feels good. And doing more independent things seems more possible now. Like it'll feel better to ask than not to ask."

The other girls had nodded.

Bicycle freed one hand from under the sheets and rubbed the fuzzy top of the cat's nose. It blinked one slow blink at her and began to purr. Bicycle thought its eyes seemed less haunted now. Their black depths swam instead with the question *What should we do today?*

This morning, the cat wasn't the only visitor in the Kosroys' apartment. Sister Wanda swept through the bedroom's curtain. "Come, my slug-a-bed girl, a beautiful day awaits. Why are you the last one up?"

Bicycle pointed to the purring lump atop her body.

"I see." The nun sat at the foot of the bed. "Cat, this is no time to doze. Everything is packed, everyone else is dressed, and Brother Otto is overseeing preparations for tonight's feast."

Sister Wanda and the monks had been so happy to hear the family was coming to visit that they'd planned out a whole three-day event, including movie nights that Daff was sure to enjoy. Sister Wanda had decided that she would personally come help shepherd the family along the bike path to the Mostly Silent Monastery. She'd arrived on her old bike yesterday.

Sister Wanda whispered conspiratorially to the cat, "Speaking of the feast, I can be persuaded to look the other way when Brother Otto decides to sneak you some choice tidbits."

The cat *mrowl*ed its approval, rose to headbutt the nun's knee, and left.

Sister Wanda smoothed the coverlet over Bicycle's legs. "I've missed you so. I'm ready whenever you are for a nice long listening session. You can tell me everything you didn't get to say over the phone. I'm sure there's more to the story of this past month than 'I taught my sisters how to ride bikes.'"

"A lot more," Bicycle agreed. She looked forward to not only telling the stories of her sisters' secret mini-adventures but also describing how Mom and Dad had handled hearing about them. The girls had spilled every detail. Yes, Mom had cried a little, but she'd also laughed, and Dad had expressed pride in the way his daughters looked out for one another. The two of them had made a deal with the girls: if Apple, Banana, Cookie, Daff, and Bicycle would be more honest about what they wanted and needed, Mom and Dad would do their best to listen and respond without letting their fears control the conversation.

Her parents also reacted better than Bicycle could have expected when she explained the whole printing of the hundred-thousand-dollar bills to rescue the Fortunes. Mom had said, "You did what you had to do to resolve an impossible situation. Can you imagine these lovely, kind bicycles being melted for scrap?" Dad had said, "It shouldn't be illegal to liberate bikes like that. I'm sure the law would make an exception for the Wheels of Fortunes if it knew they existed."

Bicycle remembered thinking that exact thought herself at the scrapyard. "I am definitely your child," she'd told them.

Cookie poked her head through the curtain. "Come on, Bicycle! The 713-C ate a twenty-pound bag of brown rice and says it will make us breakfast once we get to the bike path."

Sister Wanda squinched up her nose. "Are we eating food made by bicycles today?"

Bicycle told her, "Don't worry—the 713-C is a brilliant bike chef." It had made a shrimp scampi from some old gum a few days ago. She asked Cookie, "What's it going to make for us?"

"It says it's a surprise. I'm hungry, so get up!"

Bicycle did.

When they'd crossed the river and assembled on the bike path, Sister Wanda said a Nearly Silent blessing and made everyone check that their shoelaces were tied. Daff fiddled with the helmet cam and reminded everyone that she was making a documentary of the trip, so they should make sure they were in the shot if they did something filmworthy.

Bicycle looked at the group and saw her own excitement about the ride ahead reflected on each face. She felt pretty sure that she hadn't turned her family upside down by coming back. In fact, she might have started turning them right side up.

Cookie announced, "The 713-C would now like to present us with breakfast." She encouraged her bike, "Go ahead. I'm sure it'll be great."

The 713-C presented a tray of golden, crispy discs fragrant with maple and vanilla.

"Waffles!" Cookie crowed. "You're the best!"

Everyone chowed down.

Banana crammed a final bite in her mouth, swallowed, and started sprinting on the 713-B down the path. "Call me Banana Split, and catch me if you can!"

"Go get her!" Dad said to Apple. The haunted cat hadn't been around when they'd left Twintopia, but it bounded up the trail now. It hopped up into Apple's wicker basket, eyes wide.

Mom yelled "Slow down!" to Banana Split, then "Speed

up!" to Bicycle. The rest of the family shouted at once, pedaling hard. Sister Wanda brought up the rear, chuckling.

Bicycle watched the Fortune's odometer tick over a mile. Bicycle knew how, little by little, one mile could turn into fifty, then a hundred, then a thousand. She'd done some research with the Fortune and found out that the two-hundred-mile Katy Trail in Missouri ran close to her friends' world-famous pie shop. A three-thousand-mile trail called the Great Divide Mountain Bike Route passed right through the campus of her racer friend Zbig's new bike-racing school. Other paths crisscrossed the beautiful corners of their country and beyond, waiting to take them to meet old friends and make new ones.

She told the Fortune, "This could be the start of a lot more than one ride."

The Fortune blinked, Knock knock. It is a good one that I have been saving.

"A good one, huh? Who's there?"

Woo.

"Woo who?"

Yes, woo-hoo. I am excited as well. Woo-hoo.

Bicycle laughed. "That is a good one." She repeated, "Woo-hoo!"

Mom chimed in with her own whooping "Woo-hoo!"

So did Dad, Sister Wanda, Apple, Banana Split, Cookie, and Daff. The haunted cat put its front paws on the edge of its basket and leaned forward. The Wheels of Fortunes spit ticker tape, glowed purple messages, mumbled with a mouthful, and played a fanfare. The family and their bikes rolled down the path toward whatever adventures, great and small, lay ahead.

ACKNOWLEDGMENTS

This book had a family helping it find a place to belong from the very start.

Thank you to my wonderful team at Holiday House and my excellent editor, Margaret Ferguson, for making sure Bicycle's next story was as good as it could possibly be.

Thank you to my steadfast agent, Ammi-Joan Paquette, for encouraging me during the pandemic shutdown to try writing instead of lying on my couch eating Kit Kats. More thanks to all my super-duper-supportive writer friends at the Erin Murphy Literary Agency, who make going on social media a happy experience.

Thank you to my patient family members, who brought me Kit Kats whenever a moment was better faced with a chunk of chocolate than without, and who know that when a mother has given birth to multiples, she's going to name them whatever she wants so you'd better stop pestering her. Special thanks to my parents for asking every single person with whom they come into contact if they've purchased my books yet.

Thank you to my beloved friends, who join me in talking top-speed and also in sitting in mostly silence, letting me be who I already am.

Thank you to Storrs Library in Longmeadow, where I wrote and edited many chapters of *A Few Bicycles More* on my lunch breaks, and where my colleagues celebrate every morsel of my book news and give me Kit Kats on many Fridays.

Finally, thank you to YOU, my readers. I really do read your letters and listen to your questions, and I heard you loud and clear when you wondered where Bicycle's family has been all this time. Now you know. Write me more letters, and let's see where the next book will take us.

DON'T MISS BICYCLE'S FIRST ADVENTURE!

A TEXAS BLUEBONNET AWARD MASTER LIST BOOK

A JUNIOR LIBRARY GUILD GOLD STANDARD SELECTION

A KIDS INDIE NEXT BOOK

★ "An extraordinary pilgrimage featuring several fantastical characters and an unforgettable adventure to boot." —*Shelf Awareness*, Starred Review

★ "'Pedal headfirst' into this terrific adventure." —*Kirkus Reviews*, Starred Review

★ "The story elegantly blends elements of mystery, adventure, and fantasy." —*Publishers Weekly*, Starred Review